Ian,

Thank you for superb job of

Best Wishes

Tony & June.
Nov 2016.

Bolting Horses and Falling Bombs

The Making of a Plymouth Family, 1924 to 1945

Anthony Trevail

Strategic Book Publishing and Rights Co.

Strategic Book Publishing and rights Co.
12620 FM 1960, Suite A4-507
Houston TX 77065

www.sbpra.com

For information about special discounts for bulk purchases, please contact Strategic Book Publishing and Rights Co. Special Sales, at bookorder@sbpra.net.

ISBN: 978-1-63135-151-8

Design: Dedicated Book Services, (www.netdbs.com)

Preface

The following story is drawn on factual material, though some events and characters are fictional. Some names have been changed to protect the real identity of the persons concerned. The main characters were real people but are now sadly deceased with the exception of myself and my sister Pat. The story is presented through the eyes of a child and illustrates what life was like for a typical family before and during the Second World War in the Devon city of Plymouth, which was particularly badly hit by German bombing raids. I am grateful to my mother and father for the stories they relayed to me as I was growing up.

I would also like to thank my editor, Dr N. J. Fox, who is also my son-in-law, for his invaluable help in making my manuscript acceptable for publication.

ANTHONY TREVAIL

PLYMOUTH

JULY, 2014

Chapter 1

The hard soles of her bare feet made a sound on the blue slate pavements. There was a message repeated in each sound: 'Look after your sister.' She was terrified of the possible consequences that might be in store for her from her mother. Her vision kept blurring as fresh, salty tears came to her eyes and streaked back across her face, blown by the light summer breeze and the speed at which she was walking. Her eight-and-a-half-year-old heart was pounding away in her skinny heaving chest as she gasped for breath. But she kept going. She knew the quickest way to get home and as she came to the level crossing she prayed, 'Please God, don't let the gates be closed.' But in her heart she knew that they would be; and they were. She heard the 'chuff … chuff ... chuff' of steam from the train and went as quickly as she could up the steps of the footbridge that spanned the railway. She briefly paused to suck more air into her lungs and in a flash was off again.

She arrived at her cottage and feeling a little relieved ran sobbing through the front door. Ma had a stewpot on the kitchen range simmering away for the family's midday meal. Her younger sister Ivy and little brother Kenny were playing by the back door which led out into the large backyard. Her eldest brother Cyril was serving in the Royal Navy; eldest sister Lilian May was at work; and her other brother Eddy had just signed his Articles of Apprenticeship as an engine fitter in HM Dockyard, Devonport.

Inside the cottage, she almost collapsed, out of breath and sweating profusely, her hair sticking to her forehead. 'Ma ... Ma ... it's Vi!'

Her mother was a short dumpy woman, her body ruined by having given birth to seven children and two stillbirths. Her long dark hair was piled on top of her head and held in place by a large pin. Her clothes had seen better days but were clean. She wore a pinafore and a pair of black, worn-out, button-up boots. Her face was florid and sweaty.

'What is it Vera, what's the matter with you girl?' Vera was hysterical. 'Pull yourself together and tell me what's wrong? Where's Violet?' Vera tried to catch her breath.

'She's had an accident and they've taken her to the hospital near the Hoe.'

Ma wrung her hands in despair and said, 'Who's taken Vi? What's happened to her? If only your Pa was here.' Her husband Edward, a Canadian by birth, was serving with the Royal Marines on active service in the Dardanelles.

Vera tearfully explained all that had happened. 'She saw the flower and wanted it for you. I helped her down and held her ankles. She wriggled a bit and I couldn't hold on any longer. She slipped out and bumped on the beach. I screamed and ran down. I thought she was dead.' Vera's voice broke. The blood drained from her mother's face.

'Quick, nip next door to Mrs Daley and tell her we have to go to the hospital to see how Vi is. Ask her if she could look after your brother and sister. Now run!' Vera was out of the door in a flash.

Florrie Daley, her friend and neighbour, came round immediately. 'Lilian, I'm so sorry to hear the bad news. Of course I'll look after the little ones till you come back.'

'Thank you so much, and if I'm not home when Lilian May and Eddy come home, would you tell them to help themselves to the stew on the range?'

'Of course I will Lilian. Now off you go and I'm sure everything will be all right.'

Ma had torn off the stained pinafore that adorned her ample body, moved the stew higher from the range, grabbed her hat, coat and purse in one hand, with little Vera still sobbing in the other, and rushed off to catch the nearest tram to the hospital. Vera was made to go over in detail what had happened. The events of the day flashed before her red swollen eyes.

Vera had begged Ma to let her and Violet go for a walk on Plymouth Hoe and take a picnic, as it wasn't too far from where they lived at Anna Cottages, a terrace of four, two-up two-down, corporation cottages, just behind Union Street. She was a year and a half older than Violet, having been born in 1908. 'I'll look after Violet.'

Ma looked at her pleading daughter and said, 'Be sure that you do and be home no later than four o'clock.'

'We will, promise.'

They wore long, threadbare, hand-me-down dresses covered by a whitish, worn, cotton pinafore. Ma could not afford to buy them shoes, not in the summer, but the soles of their feet were very hard, and they did not mind one little bit. The girls waited anxiously whilst Ma made them a meagre picnic.

The day was warm and sunny, and the two sisters decided to look for wild flowers for their mother, as a surprise. On their way they had only found a few bedraggled and sunburnt flowers. Feeling disconsolate they decided to stop and eat their picnic, just past the bandstand, in the shadow of Smeaton's Tower. The grass was cool to their bare feet, so they sat down and Vera opened the small hessian bag and took out their lemonade bottle of cold tea and some bread and dripping sandwiches which had been slightly salted. From this wonderful vantage point they had a breathtaking view of the sea stretching away as far as the eye could see. There were so many things to see on the water, such as sailing boats and the motor cruisers full of holidaymakers taking trips to see the Dockyard and the warships. In the distance, past the breakwater, there was a large ship disgorging smoke from her two funnels, making the only clouds on this day.

'We haven't many flowers,' reflected Vera.

'Where shall we go after our picnic to look for some more?' asked Violet.

'Let's go down to the beach and try there,' replied Vera, looking into the distance.

They put the empty bottle in their bag and made their way slowly towards the beach. Then, about twenty yards away, something made Violet's eyes shine. Over a small wall overlooking the beach were some bright red flowers growing on a ledge out of a patch of uncultivated earth, directly above the beach.

'Look Vera, lovely red flowers!'

'We can't get them, they're too far down,' replied her sister.

'I'll climb up the wall and lean over and you hold on to my legs. But you won't let go will you?'

Vera wasn't too sure about this, but after seeing the expectant look on her younger sister's face, she nodded in agreement. Violet pulled herself up the wall and leaned over.

'Be careful,' Vera said.

The flowers were a little further down than she first thought, but certainly not out of reach. 'Hold me tight Vera, hold me.'

There was a hint of desperation in her voice as she was stretching to reach the red flowers. The beach was a long way down and her head began to swim. She felt Vera's hands losing their grip on her little legs and she slipped closer to the flowers.

'I've got some Vera,' voiced the delighted Violet, wriggling a little.

But Vera screamed above the screams of the seagulls: 'Keep still Vi, I can't hold you, you're too heavy for me!' And slipping out of her hands, her sister disappeared over the ledge.

Two fishermen who were mending their nets looked up as they heard the scream, just in time to see a small bundle land at their feet on the sand with an unpleasant thud.

'What 'ave we got 'ere? 'Tis a little maid. Hers just falled over the cliff.'

The small form lay very still and the older of the two men knelt down and put his ear to Violet's chest. 'She's breathin' Percy.'

A crowd of sunbathers ran over and made a circle around the still child. Vera had raced down the steps to the beach and run through the crowd to where her sister lay – dead, so she thought.

'That's my sister. Is she ... dead?' pointing to the lifeless form on the sand.

'No, but she's nearly a gonner. We're going to 'ave to take 'er to the 'ospital just over the top. She'll be aright, don' you worry. Was your name?'

'Vera. And that's Vi.'

The largest fisherman carefully picked up the unconscious Violet, who was like a feather in his strong sunburnt arms, and they all started to walk to the hospital. On the way Vera told them where she lived; and they told her to run home as fast as she could and to bring her mother to the hospital in Lockyer Street. Vera set off as fast as she could.

It had taken about ten minutes for the fishermen with Violet to reach the hospital, where the porter showed them into an anteroom. 'Wait here please, I'll get a nurse for you.'

Almost immediately a nurse appeared and motioned them to place Violet in a bath chair which was positioned in the corridor. She wheeled the unconscious child into another small room that smelt of carbolic soap and iodine. The fishermen explained what had happened. The nurse thanked them for their kindness and they departed.

Violet was placed very carefully on a bed and a doctor was called. As he was giving her a thorough examination he noticed that in her small right hand she was clasping a crumpled, but beautiful, red flower.

Ma was in a bad state when she arrived at the hospital with Vera. Both were out of breath, and very anxious. In the vestibule they were seen by a matron, resplendent in starched bib and hat.

'My little girl Violet, I'm her mother, how is she, please?' She clung to Vera and broke down weeping.

'There, there, now, please don't cry. Doctor says that she is going to be all right, but it might take some time.'

Apparently, Violet had now regained consciousness. The doctor had finished his examination and the diagnosis was that she had a nasty bump to the head and was partially paralysed down the left side of her body.

The sympathetic matron explained: 'Doctor thinks that she is not in grave danger, but the next few hours will be critical, and everything that can be done will be, I promise you, my dear.'

'Can I see her please?' asked Ma.

'You can see her through the glass pane in the door, but I'm afraid that's all for the moment.'

Ma looked through the door. Violet looked so small and pale, lost in the adult-sized bed; there was bandage around her head, and a nurse was in attendance. When she saw her mother through the glass panel she started to cry. Ma was devastated, and as her tears flowed she felt so helpless.

'Can I look at her Ma?' Vera pleaded, tugging at her mother's coat. Ma picked her up for a peep and Vera waved her hand at Violet. She noticed on the bedside cabinet, in a little bottle, the red flower that Violet had picked. 'Ma, that's the flower Vi picked for you, just before I let her go.' And Ma sobbed uncontrollably.

They had both looked at Violet for as long as they were allowed, before catching the tram back to Anna Cottages. By now it was getting dark. Eddy and Lilian May were waiting with Ivy and Kenny. They had all eaten their stew and the young ones were ready for bed. Lilian May blurted out, 'What's happened Ma? Mrs Daley didn't seem to know too much.'

'How is she?' asked Florrie Daley.

Ma hushed all of them and said, 'Sit down, all of you. Violet has fallen over the cliff on the Hoe and is partially paralysed, but she will get better, the doctor said. She's not out of danger, but she will survive. Lilian May, take the children up to bed, while Vera and I have some of that stew, if there's any left.'

'I'll be getting home now,' said Florrie. 'I'm so glad she'll be all right.'

'Thank you Florrie for all you have done.'

'It was no trouble at all.' And Ma saw her to the door.

Eddy ladled out some of the thick, hot, savoury, bubbly stew into two bowls. Ma and Vera began to eat, but Ma really wasn't that hungry.

The next day Violet regained some feeling in her side. She stayed in hospital for a month, which she enjoyed, especially the luxury of having a bed to herself – for she shared a bed with Vera and Ivy at home – and having more food than she ever had at the cottage. She began to put on weight and look very lovely – her blue eyes began to sparkle and shine. Someone from the family visited her as often as they could. Just before she was to be released Ma was asked to see the doctor.

'Violet is ready to go home, but she will need complete rest, Mrs Ruthven.'

'But that's not possible in our little cottage, doctor, you see there are six of us at home and she won't get any peace at all.'

'Isn't there anyone who could take her in for the recuperation period, a relative or maybe a friend?'

'How long are you talking about, Doctor?'

'Three to six months.'

'Well maybe Jim and Maggie Vincent might; they are my best friends. I will ask them and give you the answer. When does Violet need to leave the hospital?'

'Well, as soon as you can make the arrangements.'

The Vincents had been friends of the family for many years and had one son, Jimmy. They had a haulage business, well known in the Stonehouse area, and stabled their two carthorses fifty yards down the back lane from where they lived. Their house was detached, having a front garden enclosed with a wrought iron fence and gate. The backyard led on to the lane, with the lavatory situated just inside the back door. Only the three of them lived there and there were two spare bedrooms, so room wasn't a problem. Jim had been born with one leg shorter than the other and wasn't eligible for active military service.

Ma went the very next day to speak to them and it was agreed that they would take in Violet. Ma would pay a small amount towards her keep. Jimmy, who was twelve, and five years older than Violet, could never wait to tease her in one way or another whenever she visited the Vincents. Violet didn't like him very much.

On the day she was discharged she moved in with the Vincents. 'Aunt' Maggie gave her a little room in the front of the house, which was away from the stables and fairly quiet. She had a little bed, her own washstand with pitcher and bowl, which had a pretty picture painted on it. The wardrobe smelt of camphor balls, which Aunt Maggie hung near the clothes to keep the moths away. 'Uncle' had a very good library downstairs and Violet whiled away those first few weeks reading whilst regaining her strength. Ma visited a few times each week, but some of her sisters saw her more often, especially the youngest, Ivy, whom she loved best of all her siblings.

Aunt Maggie was a very good cook and Violet flourished. She gave Violet little chores to do around the house at first, just enough for a seven-year-old to accomplish. As her strength returned the chores became more rigorous. She dusted the furniture, swept the floors, cleaned the windows, of which there were many, and blackened the grate, as well as sweeping up outside. But Aunt Maggie started to suffer with her own health and placed the burden of work on Violet's shoulders, who now, most days, was left exhausted.

* * *

Six months later Ma was in the laundry room, which was used by the residents of the cottages, with Florrie Daley.

Florrie was a widow whose husband had died of consumption some three years earlier. Charlotte, her one and only thirteen-year-old daughter, was a beautiful girl with reddish hair that hung in ringlets. They were doing the family wash when a telegram boy cycled up asking for Mrs Ruthven. He handed her the telegram. She opened it with shaking hands and Florrie put her arms around her shoulders. 'What does it say Lilian? Has Edward been killed?'

'No, thank God. But he's been injured and is being repatriated. I'm so thankful that he's alive, but it doesn't say what his injuries are.' She felt faint and the colour drained from her face.

'Here Lilian, sit on this stool, I'll make us a nice cup of tea. It'll buck you up a bit. I won't be a minute.'

When she returned, Ma sipped the tea gratefully.

The following week two Royal Marine officers visited Ma and told her the terrible news. 'Please sit down Mrs Ruthven,' one of the officers said. 'I'm afraid your husband has sustained very serious injuries to his legs. There was an accident with a hand grenade and, unfortunately, the surgeons couldn't save his legs. He has lost both of them from the knees down. He's being treated in Queen Mary's Hospital, Roehampton, for limbless servicemen.'

Ma sunk down into the worn armchair and broke down crying. The family were devastated. She could not visit him as it was too far and she didn't have enough money for the train fare. They did write to each other, however. Fortunately, in due course, with two prosthetic legs, he was transferred to the Royal Naval Hospital in Stonehouse for recuperation and physiotherapy. The prosthetic legs were heavy, cumbersome and uncomfortable to wear. It was very painful for him.

The hospital was only a short distance from Anna Cottages, so the whole family were able to visit him, but he was very depressed and a mere shadow of the strapping six-foot-two Royal Marine he had been. As soon as his recuperation was complete he was to be discharged. Ma was worried about how they would manage financially. Though her husband would receive a small war pension, what job could he do with false legs?

'Who will want me, a man without legs?' he complained.

'You'll get something; you've done your bit for King and Country,' Ma said in an encouraging way. 'Perhaps the Vincents could give you work.'

'I don't want charity,' was the surly reply.

As Violet got stronger, she was being worked quite hard by Aunt Maggie, and she started to complain to her mother.

'Don't be ungrateful Vi. If they hadn't taken you in, I don't know what we should have done. Just do as you are told, and stop complaining.'

'But Ma, I get so tired and Jimmy is always on at me. Uncle Jim treats me the best.'

'Look Vi, now that your dad is home I've got enough on my plate, without you moaning. Anyway you'll be well enough to go back to school in a week or two, so you won't be working then.'

Violet returned to school. But as she got stronger, Aunt Maggie's health got worse, and this made her cantankerous, picking on Violet and piling on the work when she got home. She felt trapped with no way of escape. She ran errands for the family as well as mucking out the stables and keeping the tack in good condition. For a young girl it was exhausting work. Now that her recuperation was complete it was agreed that Ma would stop paying for her, though she would stay on at the Vincents and earn her keep. Jimmy continued to tease her whenever he got the chance and once, when Prince, one of the two black carthorses, nipped her hand as she offered him an apple, he laughed his head off.

'I hate you,' she screamed, forking some manure at him. But he just laughed all the more. She avoided him as much as possible.

* * *

Violet left school at fourteen and worked full-time for the Vincents from early in the morning to late at night. Jimmy was now nineteen and also worked full-time for his father. Aunt Maggie's health was still getting worse and she had to stay in bed a lot of the time. Violet became a full-time housekeeper, a 'skivvy without pay' as she put it, earning only her board, although now and again, if Auntie was in a benevolent mood, she gave her a few coppers to buy sweets. She also learnt how to look after the horses: grooming them, as well as continuing to keep the tack in good condition, polishing the horse brasses and mucking out the stables. Uncle Jim taught her how to use the reins and drive the drays, which she loved. She liked Uncle Jim best of all.

One cold December day he called her over. 'How would you like to drive the cart today? I've spoken to Auntie and she said it would be all right.'

'Oh, Uncle Jim I'd love to.'

Jimmy for once didn't say much and sat on the back of the cart as Violet took the reins with Uncle Jim sitting beside her. Off they went to a property in Mainstone Avenue at Cattedown. As the two men were loading furniture onto the cart, one of the horses got spooked and galloped off down the street heading straight for a group of boys playing football. All her pulling on the reins and shouting made no difference. As the horses galloped on, their hooves clattering on the cobbles, a little boy just managed to jump over a wall to get out of harm's way. A bigger boy tried to stop the horses by grabbing the reins, but he was dragged under the hooves and steel rimmed wheels and was killed. The horses came to a halt. Violet was still screaming, looking back at the crumpled body in the gutter covered in blood. Another boy, with tears streaming down his grubby face, was cradling his head and screaming: 'You've killed him.'

Uncle Jim rushed up and took Violet in his arms. 'Don't look Vi, don't look.' But she had already seen it, and the sight was engraved on her mind. She took months to get over that traumatic experience and vowed never to drive the horses again.

* * *

Violet's younger sister, Ivy, regularly visited her on Saturday afternoons. They normally went shopping in the town. They would call in to see her mother and father at Anna Cottages. Pa hadn't found work and the family were existing on what her siblings paid in keep. By now, five years had passed and Violet was growing into a beautiful, slim, young woman; her black silky hair was cut in a bob. She was nineteen years old and had been in service for eleven years. She had many arguments with Aunt Maggie, but was always reminded of how Maggie had taken her in when there was no one else. There were times when she took respite from the drudgery, especially when the men folk were out at work and Aunt Maggie was asleep upstairs in bed. She liked to relax by sitting outside, soaking up the warmth of the sun, playing with the neighbours' children and chatting to their mothers.

One warm summer day in 1928 she was outside in the front garden, sitting on the wall by the gate with her eyes closed, daydreaming. A young man of about the same age as her was striding up the street; for some reason his footsteps made her open her lazy eyes. He was wearing a uniform which she didn't readily recognise. He was very handsome, taller than her and well built. He had taken his hat off and she could see that his hair was black. As he drew near he looked her full in the face; she immediately dropped her eyelids shyly. He walked passed but stole another couple of looks at her, scratching his head in contemplation. She felt her cheeks reddening and her heart began to beat wildly in her breast. She watched him until he was out of sight, then ran indoors feeling a little faint. She thought that she recognised him, but how could she? Where did she go to see people? She racked her brain; then remembered. It was the funeral all those years ago of the boy who had been trampled by the horses. It was his best friend and he had been crying. She felt so sorry for him that she had held his hand to comfort him.

She had never had a boyfriend before and Auntie Maggie had told her that she would never have one, not whilst she was living under their roof. She couldn't get his face out of her mind and wondered if she would ever encounter him again. She didn't know why she felt so excited. Over the following days she felt as if she were walking on air and hummed and whistled whilst doing her chores. Aunt Maggie thought that young ladies who whistled were very common. They could see a difference in her whole demeanour.

'I don't know what's got into you girl, you're acting as though you've lost a farthing and found a sixpence, and I won't have it, now just get on with your work.'

'I'm so sorry Aunt Maggie.' She didn't feel sorry at all.

Chapter 2

As long as he could remember, he and his mates had been swimming under the Iron Bridge, longing for the day when they would be able to jump into the river from the bridge above. For him that day had arrived. He was hanging on for grim life, his knuckles gleaming white under his tanned skin. His heart boomed in his chest and he was breathing so quickly that his head began to swim. Thirty-five feet below him, the water was a dark green colour, allowing him to see just about a foot under the surface. Three boys, observing his predicament, shouted as one, 'Go on John, jump!'

He wished they would disappear, and that he could turn back from this mission, but he had waited such a long time for this day. He had never been so scared in his short life. Although it was a scorching summer day the metal girders on the railway bridge felt cold and clammy to his touch. The large rusty rivets stared back at him like dead eyes, daring him to jump.

'He's scared. I bet he won't do it,' shouted Alfie, the gang leader. Alfie Penrose, the biggest fourteen-year-old in the group, was a bully, and John was scared of him. 'I'll count down from ten and if you haven't jumped by then I'll push you off, so you'd better do it! Ten … nine'

John looked down at the water. His head had cleared by now, but his imagination was working overtime and he thought there was a huge eel in the murky waters, just out of sight, ready to swallow him as soon as he touched the water; or that his feet would get entangled in seaweed and drown him. His own funeral flashed before his eyes.

'Four ... three ... two.' He came to his senses. Alfie was beginning to edge his way along the bridge. 'One. I'm coming John!'

His so-called mates began to jeer and shout as Alfie got nearer. But John began to feel a steady vibration, which was getting stronger and threatened to release his clenched fists from the girder. Alfie stopped short in his tracks.

'The bloody train's coming,' he shouted in a strangled voice. There was real fear in his voice: he was on the single-track side and there wasn't room for a person and a train. John was outside the girder and relatively safe.

The bridge began to rattle and shake as Alfie quickly clambered over the girder onto the small pillar about twenty yards from where John was hanging and shaking. They could both hear the rails singing as the steam-powered goods train rumbled nearer. The driver had seen them and sounded his whistle. Fifty yards away ... thirty ... twenty ... ten. Alfie closed his eyes and used his hands and feet to stop the vibration from throwing him off the bridge. John looked at the train as it thundered by, the driver shouting, 'Stupid dunderheads!' He looked at the water below then threw himself into space. His stomach turned as he plummeted down, eyes tightly closed and arms flailing.

The water rushed up to meet him. His feet hit first and made a space for the rest of his body to fit into. The cold water filled his nostrils and his ears; he opened his eyes but did not see very much. He was slowing down; it was quiet – he couldn't hear the screeching seagulls, the jeers of his friends, the train. He was floating in a different world when, suddenly, the realisation that he had finally jumped made him laugh uncontrollably, water filling his mouth. He looked up and saw a faint light through the murky green water, gradually turning lighter until his sunburned face broke the surface. Alfie was looking down at him from the bridge and shouted, 'John did it at last.' His other mates were cheering.

'That was bloody good,' he swore back.

Alfie grimaced at him through clenched teeth, 'Think you're good do yuh? Well, we'll see about that.'

John had done it; he felt he could conquer the world. He yanked himself up the bank; his green hand-knitted, woollen, swimming trunks slipping down over his white buttocks. 'This is the best day of my life,' he roared. He had conquered Everest. Quickly grabbing his clothes he felt insouciant as he made his way home, just a short distance from the bridge.

His parents corporation house was sandwiched in the middle of a terrace. It comprised three small bedrooms upstairs, accommodating eight people. The plaster walls were painted with green distemper. All the bedrooms had basic metal framed beds with flock mattresses and striped ticking pillows. Downstairs was the front parlour, used only for special occasions and kept very tidy; sepia photographs of members of the family in silver frames adorned the mantelpiece. There was a three-seater settee and two cottage-style armchairs. A few pictures hung from the wooden picture rail. Along a narrow passage was the living room used by the whole family; also a small kitchen and scullery. Outside was a long, narrow courtyard which led into the cobbled back lane past the lavatory, a red brick construction four feet square and about six feet high with a rough wooden door. Inside, the actual lavatory had a two-foot-high brick base with a flat piece of wood with a hole in it, on top of which was a wooden hinged cover. A cast iron cistern for flushing was operated by pulling a handle at the end of a rusty chain. Hung on a nail on the inside of the wooden door by a piece of string were some rough squares of newspaper for all the family to use. Adjoining the lavatory was the washhouse. The courtyard walls, which divided the houses, were whitewashed every year, but they were crumbling with age.

John came in by way of the back lane. He couldn't wait to tell his brothers and sisters about his latest escapade. His mother had given birth to twenty-one children, eleven of whom were stillborn. Six girls and four boys survived. His three elder brothers were away in the Royal Navy but the rest of the family managed to live a spartan, yet happy life in cramped conditions.

His mother suffered very poor health and was frail, so his two elder sisters ran the house. John was the youngest by quite a few years and was spoilt by the family. His father was employed by the Gas Board earning a regular wage in difficult days. The whole family was a rumbustious group, whose merriment, good-humoured banter and noise filled the house. His sister Lucy saw him enter the scullery door. 'And what are you looking so pleased about then, John?'

'I jumped from the bridge,' he said in a stage whisper.

'I heard that,' said his mother coming into the scullery. 'You will be the death of me, you silly article. You know how dangerous it is. Why only two months ago Billy Brownlow drowned doing exactly what you've done. How many times have I told you not to do daft things; your Father will hear about this.'

'Awww Mother, don't tell Father – please!'

She continued in her verbose way until John let the words go in one ear and out the other. 'What if you had drowned, you wouldn't have been able to start your job after the holidays, now would you? Fine thing that would've been.'

'Well I didn't Mother, did I?'

'Don't you be giving me lip now.' She clipped his ear and he darted away out of reach. 'And you can take the smirk off your face too, Lucy. Tea will be ready in half an hour so don't go off anywhere.'

His mother had made pasties for their meal, one of John's favourite foods. Lucy disappeared into the kitchen smiling. John ran out to the backyard into the washhouse; he looked around furtively and, when he was sure that the coast was clear, he removed one of the red bricks in the wall and took out a brown leather pouch. Replacing the brick he ran out of the back door and off to a derelict house in the next lane, which he and his friends used as a den. The sun was still very warm and he settled himself down on an old armchair and ferreted in his pocket for the pouch. It contained a clay pipe, some tobacco and two Swan Vestas matches. He filled the bowl, tamping the tobacco down, like he had seen his older brothers do, stuck the pipe in his mouth, struck one of the matches on the wall and lit up, sucking the cool smoke into his mouth. He had been smoking for about a year, stealing little amounts of tobacco from his brothers from time to time when their backs were turned. He felt at peace with the whole world as he sucked on the stem and blew clouds of acrid, blue-grey smoke into the air. He closed his eyes and his thoughts turned to the first job he would be starting in a few weeks time. He would be earning money and would be able to buy his own tobacco.

The smoke in his mouth generated a lot of saliva and before long his mouth was full. He looked around for a likely target to direct the stream of spittle. He was a crack shot at spitting. Three feet away he spied a dried lump of dog's excrement, which had some fat blue bottles buzzing on the top. He closed one eye, took aim and the hot brown juice hit one of the flies before it could unfold its silvery wings and fly off. It struggled for a few seconds before dying in the foul smelling juice. He settled back again in the armchair, closed his eyes and started to nod off.

He awoke with a start and found himself on the ground; the armchair had been violently pulled from under him. His clay pipe lay in pieces and his tooth, which had bitten through the stem, was chipped. He felt the pain almost immediately.

'Oi! Who did that?'

'I did. So what?' shouted Alfie Penrose. He had stealthily crept up behind John and thought that it would be a good idea to dump him on the ground.

'What did you do that for? You've hurt me tooth,' shouted a very irascible John.

Alfie sneered. 'S'pose you think you're good, now you've done the jump. Well you are still the baby you were before – and I'm going to teach you a lesson.'

He started to roll up his grubby grey shirtsleeves then bunched his fists and adopted a boxer's stance. John's tooth hurt like mad. He looked at his prize pipe in pieces on the ground and his temper came bubbling to the surface, like a bottle of lemonade which has been shaken vigorously. He flew to his feet and before Alfie knew what had happened John punched him straight on the nose, which immediately spouted bright red blood which cascaded onto his dirty shirt. Alfie made a kind of bellowing sound, which turned into weeping, his eyes filling with tears that coursed down his grubby cheeks leaving clean trails. John could not believe what he had just done, and as an act of bravado pointed his finger in Alfie's face and said in an authoritative manner, 'Don't you ever touch me again.'

John strolled home, a very happy victor. Alfie, still bawling, held a dirty piece of rag to his nose to stem the blood and made his way home. After that incident Alfie had respect for John, and in time they became firm friends.

* * *

Two years had now passed by, and the boys were sixteen. John had been with the water board for two years as an apprentice turncock. Alfie did not have a proper job but helped out where he could to earn a shilling or two. December was bitterly cold. Everyone was finding it very difficult to keep warm. All the houses had open coal fires, but the majority of the people in John's street did not have enough money to buy coal, or what they were able to buy was eked out by being burnt in one room only where the whole family would spend the evening, trying to keep warm. John was fortunate to have a uniform, which was supplied for his job, and this included a stout pair of hob-nailed boots, which kept him reasonably warm and dry.

Times were very hard and many men were out of work. It was pitiful to see them hanging around on street corners in small groups, burning wood in a brazier to keep warm. One Saturday afternoon, a group of boys were playing football in John's road. The ball was an inflated pig's bladder which someone had acquired from the local abattoir. Further up the road a family was being evicted and their furniture was being loaded onto a cart drawn by two huge black carthorses.

A pretty dark-haired girl of about thirteen was up in the seat holding the reins. She looked very unhappy concerning the plight of the family being turned out. The small children were stood with their mother while the father remonstrated with the bailiff: 'You can't throw us out, we haven't anywhere to go. How about me children an' me wife? We'll all starve.'

The barrel-chested and uncaring bailiff, with his blood-red face replied, 'You can't pay your rent. You've got to go.'

The neighbours became very angry and a crowd gathered quickly. John and Alfie were outside John's house observing what was going on. Suddenly, the football struck one of the stallions, who took fright and tried to rear up, but was unable to, due to the harness; this spooked the other horse and, as one, they began to bolt down towards John and Alfie, neighing loudly. The girl on the cart screamed and pulled on the reins, but she wasn't strong enough.

'Look out! The horses are bolting,' someone shouted.

They galloped with nostrils flared and the white of their eyes turned up in their heads behind the black leather blinkers; steel rimmed wheels and metal hooves made a deafening noise on the cobbles. They were heading towards the children playing football.

John and Alfie dashed to get the children out of the way, pushing them over the small walls in front of the houses. There was one little boy rooted to the spot just yards away from the demented beasts. With superhuman effort Alfie ran and grabbed the boy and pushed him out of harm's way then, in a foolhardy but brave act, made a grab for the reins. The girl had let them go and was clinging on for dear life, her face ashen. Alfie was lifted off his feet like a flying leaf and buffeted on the flanks of the stallion.

'Hold on Alfie,' bawled John; but Alfie was thrown in the air like a rag doll and fell under the steel-shod hooves and metal-bound wheels of the runaway cart. He let out a blood-curdling yell as he tumbled into the gutter, bleeding profusely from his head.

The cart and horses now slowed a little and the girl fought once more to bring them under control. John ran to Alfie's side. 'He's dead. I know it.' He cradled Alfie's blood-stained head in his arms and rocked him to and fro, moaning to himself, tears running down his florid face. A crowd gathered quietly around the tragic pair. Some tried consoling John, but he kept on wailing. An ambulance was called for and Alfie's body was transported to the hospital at Green Bank.

His funeral was held soon after, which was attended by a huge gathering of people from the neighbourhood. John kept his emotions under control until he looked down at the coffin and threw some dirt onto it. Then he burst into tears, before walking away and weeping bitterly by a leafless tree. He had lost the best friend a boy could have. A young girl came up to him and held his hand to comfort him. 'Please don't cry.' It was the girl on the cart.

Chapter 3

In September 1924 John reported for work at Plymouth Barbican replenishing French fishing trawlers with water and blocks of ice to keep the fish fresh. After four years he obtained another job based at the Town Hall where he was employed by Plymouth City Water Works. His work now took him to private houses and concerned rectifying plumbing problems, such as changing tap washers and investigating water leaks which customers had reported. He also had to do night duties which entailed listening for water leaks in the quiet of the night using sounding sticks. He was now twenty and still lived with his parents in Cattedown, an area near the Barbican.

One day, whilst walking down a street, he happened to notice a very pretty, dark-haired girl of about the same age as him. She was sitting on the wall at the bottom of a large garden enjoying the sunshine. He assumed she lived there, and felt an immediate attraction. Since the age of sixteen he had courted a few girls, but none had been serious liaisons. This girl looked different and bore a fragile look. She glanced up as he came nearer and gazed into his eyes, which were the greyest she had ever seen. He smiled and she blushed, lowering her gaze. He kept looking at her as he approached and, as he drew near, she diffidently returned his look. His heart missed a beat and as he passed her he looked back over his shoulder, in time to see her disappear indoors. His rubicund cheeks burned with excitement as his heart pounded in his chest. He thought he had seen that face before somewhere. For the rest of his journey home, she was the only thought in his head.

His behaviour changed a little, though only his mother sensed that a young woman was the cause. John didn't see this girl again for some months as the weather was very inclement, there being many days of summery torrential rain.

On a few occasions Violet had looked through Aunt Maggie's lace curtains hoping to see John walking by. Aunt Maggie had caught her daydreaming and chided her. 'Stop dreaming Vi, and get on with your work, you're wasting valuable time!' Auntie was much older now and still as cantankerous as ever.

'You are a slave driver Auntie.'

'How dare you say that after all I've done for you?'

Violet's life was miserable, but she felt incumbent to do the best that she could for her Aunt. She only had her parents to turn to for solace, though her sisters were kind and helpful.

One day as she was doing her chores there was a knock at the door.

'Violet, answer the door, will you?' said Auntie.

John was about to rap again when the door opened and 'the girl' was standing in front of him. 'I've come to mend the tap, it's leaking isn't it?' John exclaimed.

'You'd better come in,' said Violet, her heart almost bursting.

'Who is it?' Auntie asked curtly.

'The man to mend the leaking tap.'

'Tell him to wipe his boots.'

'You'd better do as Auntie says,' cautioned Violet. 'She's not in very good health and can be quite cantankerous.'

Violet led John down the long passage into the scullery where a tap was leaking. 'I'll change the washer, that should do it. Do you want to fill the kettle, because I'll have to turn the water off?'

'It's all right, we've got a full kettle on the range. Would you like a cup of tea?'

John nodded. Auntie was hovering in the background.

'Well go on then, make the man his tea,' croaked Auntie. 'And bring mine up to my room; I'm not feeling too good.'

Violet busied herself as John went outside to turn off the water and set to work on the tap. She took her Aunt's tea upstairs. 'Here you are Auntie, where shall I put it?'

'Just put it on the side table; and don't go annoying the workman, just let him get on.'

'How would I annoy him Auntie?'

'By chatting too much.'

Violet put the cup on the small table and went downstairs. 'Do you take milk and sugar?' she asked, coming into the scullery.

'Please, and two spoons of sugar, if you can manage it?'

'You certainly like it sweet. Do you mind if I watch you work?' she asked, mindful of Auntie upstairs.

'Not at all, I'd like that.' There was a pause, then he said, 'I feel that I recognise you from somewhere.'

'I don't know where. I never go anywhere.'

'Your face seems familiar.'

And then it came to them: the funeral of Alfie Penrose. 'You were the girl on the cart.'

'Yes, and I held your hand when you were crying.'

'Well I wasn't very old and they were burying my best friend Alfie.'

John purposely took his time over replacing the tap washer and over the next hour they conspiratorially exchanged some family history. Violet was whispering so that Auntie wouldn't overhear. But then she shouted down the stairs, 'What's taking so long?'

'I've finished Mrs Vincent,' John replied.

'About time too. I'll come down and pay you.'

'Please don't bother to come downstairs, because you'll get an invoice from Plymouth Corporation Water Works through the post.'

'Oh all right. Thank you.'

John and Violet had warmed to each other and John said that, whenever he was passing, he would look out for her. She said that she would try to look out for him. Over the coming months they got to know each other better, and one day in October he got up the courage to ask her out. He knew that she had never been out with a man before.

'I'm not sure that Auntie would approve,' she said nervously. 'Well I can ask her.'

'Would you?'

'Of course I will. I'll go and get her now.'

And, miracles of miracles, Auntie reluctantly agreed, but added, 'You are to bring her home by eleven o'clock and no later, or there will be trouble.'

'Of course I will Mrs Vincent.'

'Oh, thank you Aunt Maggie.'

Violet's blue eyes shone with pure joy. They decided they would go to the pictures.

* * *

John waited outside the Empire cinema at seven o'clock. He felt a little self-conscious, waiting in the glare of the lights. It was drizzling and he was wearing his one and only blue suit, a white shirt and a red tie. Over this he wore a grey mackintosh with a grey trilby hat. It was quite dark and he peered at every woman who passed by wondering if she was his beautiful Violet. Suddenly, there she was; and his heart was beating furiously. She looked stunning; it took his breath away.

Two hours earlier Violet's younger sister Ivy had come across from her parent's house to help her get ready for her very first date. Up in her bedroom she was giving Violet some tips about make-up. 'Put some rouge on Violet.'

'Do you think I ought? What will Auntie say?'

'Don't worry about her.'

'How about Uncle Jim and Jimmy, what will they think?'

'Do you want to look nice or not?' retorted Ivy. 'Anyway you can slip out without them seeing you.'

'Of course I want to look my best, but it'll be a hard job.'

'Vi, you are beautiful and you don't know it.'

'I don't know where I'm supposed to be beautiful.'

'You have beautiful eyes and you are slim.'

Ivy dressed her in a floral patterned frock with a small angora stole over the top. She wore her sensible shoes, put on her light raincoat and a pretty hat held on with a pin. As it was raining she borrowed one of Auntie's umbrellas.

Her younger sister Ivy was also a real beauty, with short natural blonde hair and an hourglass figure. Boys had been after her since her school days; she had some experience with men and was an outrageous flirt.

'You'll get yourself into trouble one of these days, teasing the boys, Ivy!' remarked Violet.

'Don't worry your pretty head over me, I can look after myself. Now hurry up or you'll be late. And tell me all about it soon, promise?'

'Of course I'll tell you all about it.'

She saw John waiting for her outside the cinema before he saw her and thought he looked very handsome.

'We'll go in the one and threes, if that's all right with you?' said John. To her they were the posh seats.

They held hands all through the film and stole glances at each other in the dark. Neither could concentrate on the film. It had stopped raining when they got outside. John bought fish and chips, which they ate from the newspaper as they walked back to Violet's house. Violet felt so happy. It was the best day of her life so far. He got her home by quarter to eleven. They went in the front gate, through the garden and up to the front porch. He took her in his arms and kissed her; she thought she would faint. She could taste the grease from the battered fish they had eaten earlier, but didn't mind one bit.

They met many times over the next year and fell madly in love with each other. Auntie liked John, as did the rest of the family, even Jimmy.

* * *

John bought a second-hand tandem which he and Violet used for summer evening rides to the beach and Dartmoor.

For both of them, life was wonderfully insouciant. Violet's sister Vera had moved to Nottingham, her three brothers were all serving in the Royal Navy, her other sister Lilian May had moved to another part of the city, whilst her younger sister Ivy had moved into a small flat with her friend Ruby. Her mother and father were the only ones now living in Anna Cottages.

They had been courting for well over a year; but Violet was finding life unbearable working for Auntie. She had spoken to John about this on many occasions and John in turn had spoken to his parents. John's brothers and sisters had all married and left home, and the house was quite empty with just him and his parents living there. She could have moved back to her parents' cottage but felt that she had been away for so long that it would not be fair to them, now that they had it to themselves. John asked his parents if they would take her in as a lodger. They agreed and invited her to stay with them providing that she found herself a job and paid her way. She readily said that she would look for work as soon as she left the Vincents'.

Aunt Maggie was very upset when Violet informed her of her decision to move. John was there beside her, supporting her.

'How will I manage without you?' she cried.

'I'm sorry Auntie, but I am an adult now and I need to make a new life for myself. Perhaps Uncle Jim could pay for someone to help with the work here.'

'But they won't work like you do,' she whined.

'You never appreciated me,' Violet replied. 'I wished you had given me some praise for the way I worked for you, but you never did, not once, and now that I'm going, you're saying that I was a good worker. Well, it's too late. I'm definitely leaving.'

When Auntie realised that Violet was adamant (she had previously always been so taciturn), she wished them the best for the future and said that Jimmy would move her things to John's house. Jimmy harnessed the horses and, with John's help, loaded the few sticks of furniture that Violet had accumulated over the twelve years that she had lived there.

Violet was very fortunate and found work at a sweet factory, which paid poorly, but was something. She helped John's mother after work, doing the things that she was good at and had been doing since the age of seven and a half: cooking, cleaning and generally running a house. John's mother was still in poor health and was glad of the help. She treated Violet like a daughter, who was enjoying family life for the first time. In the dark, cold evenings of that first winter, the four of them played cards and board games, or just sat around the fire listening to the wireless. Occasionally John took Violet to his local pub, The Morely Arms, where he liked a pint of beer; Violet just drank shandy. She felt uncomfortable in the pub, but went because she loved John so much.

When they got home they would sit by the dying embers in the grate and John would always have his last pipe of the day. He had not ceased his habit of spitting tobacco juice, but now he spat it into the fire, where it would hiss and sizzle and dance around like quicksilver on the hot hearth. This habit repulsed Violet's senses. She had to dig off the hardened residue from the fire in the mornings, and it turned her stomach. But John didn't think it was disgusting at all because he had always done it and his family had put up with it for years. They indulged him in this degrading act, saying, 'The fire party is in action again!' (He never gave up this abominable habit.)

Chapter 4

Violet's eighteen-year-old sister Ivy and her flat mate Ruby were relaxing with a drink after three dances in a row. They were never short of admirers.

'I'm hot Ruby, I need to go outside for a breath of fresh air.'

'I'll wait for you here, but don't be too long.'

Ruby was short and buxom with auburn hair. Her best feature was her teeth which were white and straight. When she smiled she twisted the boys around her little finger. Ivy's long blonde hair cascaded down to her shoulders and had a natural wave in it. Her dress clung to her voluptuous body and her stiletto shoes showed off her slender legs to wonderful effect. She had grown into a really beautiful woman.

As she walked towards the door leading onto the veranda and the cool of the night a few young men watched her; she always drew the attention of men. Jack Lambert had been watching Ivy for most of the evening. He took a deep drag on his Woodbine and watched the exhaled smoke rising towards the mirrored ball suspended from the ceiling. He had not been to the Corn Exchange for a few years, but thought that he had seen Ivy once or twice before, but couldn't place where. He admired her skill as a dancer as he was quite an expert himself; he had taken lessons. He was wearing his blue pinstriped suit, a polka-dot silk tie under a rounded starched collar. His patent leather dancing shoes were buffed to a high polish. His wavy dark brown hair was parted on the left and slicked down with brilliantine, which gave it a rich deep lustre. He had liberally splashed himself with cologne. He had rugged good looks and a taut muscular body. His teeth were white and even and he thought of himself as a ladies man; he had never been short of girlfriends. He had been leaning against the bar supping a pint of beer, but now he casually made his way towards the balcony, drink in hand. Ivy sensed that someone had joined her, but did not look. He glanced at her left hand to see if she was wearing a ring; she wasn't. Jack had the gift of the gab and spoke to her.

'Good evening, I noticed you earlier. Where did you learn to dance like that?'

Ivy looked at Jack and liked what she saw. 'I've had lessons,' she answered.

'Yes, I thought so, me too. I've taken lessons,' replied Jack. 'Would you care to have the next dance with me? Oh, by the way, my name is Jack.'

'And I'm Ivy,' she answered. 'Yes, I'd be delighted.'

The six-piece band struck up a tango as Jack led Ivy onto the dance floor. Ruby was there already and noticed Jack and Ivy as they came on. 'He looks nice,' she thought, much better than the one I'm dancing with.

Jack and Ivy moved as one. Ivy realised that he was a wonderful dancer as they swayed to the tune of 'Jealousy', Jack's favourite. He guided her this way and that and she followed his every move. The other dancers noticed the wonderful display and moved to the outside of the floor to watch this show of artistry and movement. The spotlight was following them around. Ivy felt exhilarated. Her brow glistened with perspiration and her scent wafted into Jack's nostrils. When the music ended, the crowd showed their appreciation by clapping. Jack led her back to her table and asked if he might join her. Ruby came back and sat down. Ivy introduced Ruby to Jack.

'Can I offer you a drink, ladies?' asked Jack.

Ruby quickly replied in an attempt at a posh voice, 'I'll have a pink gin, and can you make it a large one, I'm rather thirsty?'

'And you Ivy?'

'Oh, I'll have the same as Rube, but just an ordinary one, please.'

Jack thought to himself that Ivy had manners but that Ruby didn't have decorum. 'Won't be a tick,' he said and made his way to the bar.

'What do you think of him Rube? Fancy asking him for a large one! You are cheeky.'

'He looks as though he can afford a large one. He looks all right, I suppose.'

'Coo, he's a real smasher! He can certainly dance,' Ivy said.

Jack returned with their drinks and sat down.

'Thanks very much, I'm sure,' Ruby said, taking a long sip.

'Yes thanks very much,' echoed Ivy. 'I haven't ever seen you here before. Where do you normally go dancing?'

'I go where the fancy takes me, but I have been here many times,' he replied nonchalantly.

Jack and Ivy danced the night away and were really enjoying themselves. At half past eleven Ruby intimated that they should be leaving.

'I'll give you a lift home if you both like,' offered Jack. 'Do you live far away?'

'No, not too far,' they said in unison.

They could not believe their ears, a good-looking man with a car. They passed in their tickets to the cloakroom attendant and retrieved their coats, then all three made their way out into the night air.

'Where is it parked Jack?' asked Ivy.

'Just around the corner, not far.'

They turned the corner. 'I can't see a motor car,' said Ruby.

'Who said anything about a car,' he replied sardonically.

The only machine they saw was a gleaming motorcycle and sidecar. 'Is that it?' asked Ivy.

'I'm not going home in that!' exclaimed Ruby.

Ivy said, 'Oh come on, it will be such fun.'

Ruby reluctantly squeezed into the sidecar and Ivy sat pillion. Jack donned his peaked hat, turned around the wrong way, and put his goggles on the top. He pulled on his leather gauntlets and kicked his gleaming Royal Enfield 350 cc into life. 'Hang on tightly!'

They sped off with Ivy clinging to Jack's waist with all her strength and Ruby's head bobbing up and down like a cork on a rippling stream. She screamed at Jack to slow down. They soon arrived outside the flat and Ruby staggered out of the sidecar cursing Jack, her legs shaking. The colour had drained from her face and Jack could see that she was mad with him.

'I'll never go in that boneshaker again, not for all the tea in China.' Before he could apologise she ran into the flat.

'I think you've upset Ruby,' Ivy said with a smile on her lips.

'I didn't mean to, but did you like the ride, Ivy?' he said, with an air of pride.

'Oh I loved it Jack.'

He switched off the ignition and dismounted, helping Ivy down from the pillion seat. 'I'll walk you to the door.'

Her heart was beating wildly as they walked slowly to her door. They talked for some while and she told him that she worked in a sweet factory with Ruby. Her sister Violet had helped her get the job. They stopped and looked at each other. Jack touched her cheek with the back of his hand and then traced the outline of her full lips with his finger. She was about to say something but Jack prevented her, pressing his fingers more firmly against her lips. His left hand embraced the nape of her neck and his right hand encircled her small waist. She felt light headed and thought her heart would burst. Jack was very excited and with his gaze fixed on her moist red lips he slowly brought his lips against hers in a long lingering kiss. She was breathless. 'I'll have to be going in now Jack.'

'Please stay a little longer, Ivy,' his voice was urgent.

'No I must go now.' She broke away and took her key out.

'When will I see you again, Ivy. I've just got to. You can phone me at work, if you have a pencil and paper, I'll give you the number.'

He had just finished his apprenticeship as a trimmer at Bartons Motor House on Mutley Plain, where he upholstered seats for the motorcars. He had a very inventive mind and was always trying out new ways to make money. In his spare time he bought second-hand motorcycles and restored them, always selling at a profit. He was thought of as a bit of a spiv.

'Here you are,' said Ivy. She gave him the paper and pencil. With that she turned the key and went in. She shut the door and leaned against it feeling so excited. She would be phoning Jack but not for a few days. 'Don't be too keen,' she said aloud.

Ruby was asleep when she got upstairs. Jack drove to his house in North Road where he lived with his parents and brother George. The house was quiet and he went straight to bed. But he couldn't get to sleep because his mind was filled with visions of Ivy.

Ivy did not ring Jack that week and he was very disappointed. He decided to go to the dance on Saturday and see if she would be there. He saw Ruby dancing with a rough looking man, but there was no sign of Ivy. (She had stayed in because she was suffering from a bad cold.) When the dance finished he made his way towards Ruby to enquire where Ivy was. But Ruby was not pleased to see him.

'Where's Ivy tonight, Ruby?' Ruby thought that she would stir up a little trouble, partly because she did rather like Jack, and partly because he wasn't interested in her.

'She's not interested in seeing you!'

'Why not?' Jack replied with surprise in his voice.

'I'm just not saying.'

'Will you pass on a message to her, please?'

'Sorry I can't do that.'

'But why not?'

She ignored him and turned to the rough man that she was with. Jack caught her arm.

'Please Ruby would you just pass on a message to Ivy for me?' She ignored him and turning to the man she was with said, 'Sid, will you tell this man to stop bothering me?'

'You heard what the lady said, now get lost mate.' He was over six feet tall and well built.

'I only…' And that was as far as Jack got. Sid grabbed Jack by his silk tie and, twisting it, pulled his face closer. Jack could smell the other's foul breath. Sid hissed, 'I said push off mate and leave my girlfriend alone.'

A few people looked in the direction of the commotion. Sid was enjoying himself.

'I don't want any trouble, just asking Ruby to do me a favour. Now please take your hands off me.' Jack gasped as Sid twisted his tie tighter.

'And what if I don't? What are you going to do, you little pipsqueak?'

Ruby was grinning. Suddenly Sid's eyes took on a glassy look as Jack's bunched fist smashed into his jaw breaking it. He crumpled to the beer stained floor. Ruby screamed as Jack calmly straightened his tie, neatened himself up and sauntered towards the exit. Although he was feeling down at not getting anywhere with Ruby, he was euphoric at the demise of Sid and dismissed the pain in his right hand as being of little consequence. He had been boxing since he was sixteen and could handle himself well.

* * *

Ruby went with Sid to the hospital where the doctor diagnosed he had a broken jaw. He couldn't speak but the looks he threw Ruby and his gesticulations made her realise that he was raging at what Jack had done to him and that she was the cause. They were keeping him in overnight and said that he would have to be operated on the next day.

Ruby went back to the flat. Ivy was still in bed suffering from her cold, but was awake and wanted to know if Jack had been at the dance. Ruby looked drained and said, 'Jack has only been and put Sid in hospital.'

'What do you mean? How? What's happened?'

'Jack got in a fight with him and punched him on the jaw. He's going to have an operation in the morning.'

Ivy looked shocked but said, 'I know what Sid is like; he's a bully and at last he got his comeuppance. I bet he started it.'

Ruby started to cry. 'It was all my fault. I wouldn't tell Jack why you weren't at the dance and he wanted me to bring you a message. We had a little argument and then Sid grabbed him by his tie.'

'I knew it wasn't Jack's fault. I bet he won't want to see me again now. I met someone nice and you were jealous.'

'I'm sorry Ivy, I wasn't to know that it would end the way that it did. Sid won't want anything to do with me again, I know that.'

'I'm reluctant to say this, but you deserve all that you get,' replied Ivy, snuffling into her handkerchief.

'Well I'm going to bed. I've had enough for one night,' said Ruby. And she left Ivy and made her way to her bedroom.

* * *

The only way that Jack could see Ivy was to go to her address. The next day, Sunday, at one o'clock he drove down to her house and, after parking the bike, knocked on her door. She answered it wearing her dressing gown.

'Jack!' she exclaimed, 'I've got an absolute stinker of a cold.'

Jack could see that she wasn't well. He explained what had taken place the night before. She said that Sid was in Freedom Fields Hospital, with a broken jaw. Jack looked surprised. 'I didn't think that I hit him that hard, but he did deserve it you know.'

'Yes, Ruby explained everything.'

'When can I see you again Ivy?'

'I'll be better in a few days, I'm sure.'

'Can I see you then?'

'Shall we go to the dance next Saturday?' she suggested.

'Fine. And then on Sunday we could go for a ride out on the bike across the moors. What do you say?'

'Oh, I'd love that Jack.'

'I'll pick you up at seven o'clock then.' He blew her a kiss and drove home feeling happy.

Saturday took a long time to come, or so it seemed to them both. Ivy took her time getting ready. Her make-up was perfect and she looked lovely. She shrugged on her low-waist, peach, silk dress that had frills around the bodice and hem. The frills jiggled with every movement. She tied a scarf around her forehead and finished off with a double row of imitation pearls. She wore her high heels and dabbed some 'Evening in Paris' perfume behind her ears and on her wrists. She smelt divine.

Jack had but one pinstriped suit and only wore it when he went anywhere special. Ivy was listening for the sound of his motorbike and, when she heard him pull up outside, her heart missed a beat. He looked incredibly handsome. She got into the sidecar and put the lid down so that the wind wouldn't spoil her hairdo. He drove more sedately to the dance hall and parked a short distance away. He bought the tickets and they made their way to the cloakrooms, where they left their outer coats.

They abandoned themselves to dancing and laughed and talked the whole time. During the last waltz she put her arms around his neck and he put his arms around her slim waist, and their bodies came close together. Her eyes were closed and she felt as though they were the only ones there. Then she opened her eyes and met his; he kissed her, hungrily, a French kiss, with his mouth open. No one had ever kissed her like this before and her head started to spin. She thought she might faint. He had kissed many girls like this but this kiss was unbelievable.

'Oh Jack, I think I'm falling for you.'

'And me with you Ivy.'

This was the beginning of a wonderful relationship.

Jack had changed his bike for a Harley Davidson WL45, that had the new V-twin engine. It had a top speed of sixty-eight miles per hour and had come all the way from America. This was Jack's pride and joy. The problem was that it only had one seat, so Jack had had to make a pillion seat with footrests.

He picked Ivy up the next day, at one o'clock, and they rode across Roborough Down on their way to Yelverton, before continuing out to the Plume of Feathers pub at Princetown for lunch. No one had treated Ivy like this before and she hoped that it would go on forever.

In time, she introduced him to her mother and father who were still living in Anna Cottages. They liked him very much and when he asked Mr Ruthven for her hand in marriage, the reply was, 'Certainly, certainly.' Jack bought her a lovely diamond engagement ring, surrounded by sapphires. They had a wonderful courtship and travelled everywhere on the Harley. Jack changed his job and worked at the Milehouse Bus Depot, making bus seat covers. Ivy continued to work at Tucketts, the local sweet factory. Her elder sister Violet and John often made up a foursome and enjoyed their free time together.

In July 1936 Jack and Ivy were married. Ivy wore a white satin dress and satin high-heeled shoes and carried an enormous bouquet of red roses. Her lacy headdress reached down to her ankles. Jack looked splendid in a single-breasted grey pinstriped suit and he wore a white rose in his buttonhole. She looked delightful in her little dress, carrying a posy of pink flowers and wearing leaves entwined around her head. It was a lovely wedding.

Chapter 5

After about a year John proposed marriage to Violet and, in spite of her abhorrence of his spitting, she loved him dearly and accepted him as he was. He bought her a beautiful engagement ring of one large diamond surrounded by a cluster of small diamonds. It was second-hand, bought from the pawnbrokers. Violet loved it and in turn bought John a signet ring with his initials engraved upon it. They celebrated their engagement at the Morley Arms with Ivy and Jack.

Six months later Violet's mother died. She was forty-nine years old and had been a diabetic for the last twenty years. Violet and all the family were devastated and her funeral was held at Weston Mill Cemetery. Her father took it very badly and his health started to deteriorate. He moved from Anna Cottages to a small flat near to where Violet and John lived, in Cattedown.

On 16 January 1932 John and Violet were married at the Plymouth Register Office. Ivy was her maid of honour and Jack was the best man. John had taken a few days off work and the honeymoon was spent on day trips because money was tight. Violet's father continued to ail and she took him food daily as he had seemed to have given up the will to live.

'You must look after yourself pa. Look, I've brought you a lovely cottage pie, your favourite.'

'That's very kind of you Violet, but what's the point? I've got nothing to live for now that ma's gone. She did everything for me ever since I came back from the war.'

'John and I will look after you now, so don't worry.'

'I just miss her so much.'

'We all do pa, but you need to get your strength back. Then you will feel better.'

Violet asked John whether he would mind moving in with her father, to look after him for a while to build him up. He agreed and they moved in. Violet looked after her father full-time and, gradually, he began to pick up. The neighbour, a widow called Joyce, was very kind to her father. She visited him daily and they built up a wonderful friendship. (Over the next year Violet's father made a complete recovery and fell in love with Joyce. They decided to move to St. Austell in Cornwall, where Joyce had been brought up.)

Now that Joyce was seeing to her father she and John decided they could move out, but not back to John's parents' house. They really wanted to be on their own and started looking for a flat. They found one in Mainstone Avenue, just a 'baccy spit' from his parents. It comprised a small sitting room, a kitchen, a bedroom and an outside lavatory. They managed to furnish it with second-hand furniture and the bits and pieces that Violet had brought from the Vincents'.

December was very cold and, one day after work when John got home, Violet had a strange look on her face as he sat down for his evening meal of tripe and onions, one of his favourite meals.

'That looks good enough to eat, Vi. What's up with you, you're looking a little strange?'

'We are going to have a baby!' she exclaimed.

John almost choked. 'We are going to have a baby, are you sure?'

'Almost. I've missed my period.'

'When will it be due?'

'Next July if I'm right.' John walked around the table and picked her up bodily and started swinging her around. 'Put me down John, you have to be careful.'

'Oh, of course. I'm going to be a father!'

'I will have to knit baby clothes and we will have to get a crib and we will…'

'Steady on Vi.' He pulled her to himself and kissed her tenderly.

'Aren't you the clever one?'

'Well, you had something to do with it,' she replied.

They talked of nothing but the baby for the rest of that evening. Over the coming months, she knitted many baby clothes and he made a cot out of spare timber that he had obtained from his workmates.

On 28 July 1933 Violet went into a long and difficult labour at the City Hospital and gave birth to her first daughter, who weighed six and a quarter pounds. They decided to call this little bundle of joy Jean. John wasn't allowed to be in attendance at the birth, but saw her the next day. He was very excited as he was shown into the room where Violet was breastfeeding her baby. She looked up at John, 'Isn't she beautiful?'

'She's the spitting image of you Vi. The same eyes and nose. Can I hold her?'

'As soon as I've finished feeding her. She's a hungry girl.'

John kissed his wife, put his arms around her and gazed at his little baby.

A nurse put her head around the door and announced, 'Ten more minutes and then you will have to leave.'

John just had time to hold his daughter for a few minutes, before kissing Violet goodbye. 'I do love you Vi,' he said tenderly. 'And I must wet the baby's head.'

He still liked his beer very much and that evening he staggered home having drunk too much. Violet was in hospital for ten days and John was 'tiddly' –his term for being a little drunk – on more than one occasion before she came home. They both felt that the flat at Mainstone Avenue wasn't the ideal place to bring up a child, because it was rather damp; so they looked for somewhere else.

Over the next two years they moved twice, and then good fortune struck. Mr Crocker, a reservoir keeper at Rowdens Reservoir in Stoke, was retiring from the Plymouth Corporation Water Works and John applied for his job and got it. He and Violet were over the moon about this and in 1934 they moved in. Uncle Jim came with Jimmy and moved their belongings to the cottage. However, this good news was tarnished by the fact that John's mother had developed cancer and died suddenly. She was sixty-two years old. The funeral was a very sad event, but well attended.

This reservoir had been built in 1878 and stood in two to three acres of land, the bulk of the space being taken up with the actual reservoir itself. The grounds were entered through magnificent, seven-foot-high, wrought iron gates painted 'water-works green', which were slung between two huge Dartmoor granite pillars. A thirty-yard path with raised borders either side led to the small cottage. A small porch led into the dining room, next to which was the sitting room. The scullery was tucked under the stairs and had a small window looking out to the path which led into Cundy's fields. John fitted a gas cooker under the stairs, where Violet had to do all the baking and cooking. The space was so small that only one person could use the cooker. A large pantry was next to it with fitted shelves, and a metal gauze screen let in air, which circulated to keep the food cool.

The sitting room walls were distempered green, which was easy on the eyes. There was a sash window above a window seat from which one could look out over the front of the property. They acquired a 'three-piece suite' which fitted well in the room. Violet hung a print of 'The Boyhood of Raleigh' over the mantelpiece, upon which stood a French clock that had a glass front with a hand painted picture showing a dog with its tail between its legs, cowering by its master, who was holding a shotgun and had some birds tied around his waist. There was a green tiled Devon fireplace. The crockery and cutlery were all basic and mainly bought second hand or given as wedding presents. Violet had a treadle-operated Singer sewing machine, which she placed in front of the window so as to gain as much light as possible when using it. There was a glass-fronted display cabinet in which was placed a biscuit barrel with a wicker handle and a cut glass decanter with six matching glasses, as well as the best crockery. John had sawn the legs down on one of the chairs so that Violet could attend to Jean easily.

Just inside the front door was a telephone, which had a line to the offices of the waterworks. It consisted of a polished mahogany box with a black Bakelite mouthpiece and earpiece. Two brass bells sat on the top and turning a small handle on the side operated it. A flight of fourteen stairs led up to two double bedrooms. At the top of the stairs was a small window measuring one foot wide by two foot long, which looked out over the back lane and the fields and in the distance Dartmoor. In their bedroom they had a double iron bedstead with a feather mattress and the cot, which John had built. Violet put an enamel pail with a lid at the bottom of their bed, so that they could use it in the night. This was to save having to go to the outside lavatory. The other bedroom was unfurnished as yet.

Outside and attached to the wall at the back was the lavatory. The door was green and the inside walls were whitewashed. Squares of newspaper were hung on a rusty nail hammered into the wall. Just opposite the lavatory a stable door opened into the wash house. A coalbunker stood in one corner and a brick built copper boiler for washing clothes stood in the other corner.

John led Violet and Jean through a green wooden door which opened up to a steep gravel strewn path, whose walls were covered in cotoneaster and ivy. On reaching the top they beheld a panoramic vista, from Dartmoor in the east to Plymouth Sound in the west. On a clear day the Eddystone Lighthouse would be visible.

'John, what a wonderful place. I just can't believe our luck. We are going to be very happy here all right. But will you be able to manage everything? It all looks so complicated.'

'I'm sure I shall manage. Mr Crocker gave me a lot of information about the running of everything.' Violet was reassured by his reply.

The reservoir itself was ring shaped and rose out of the ground by fifteen feet. A wide grassy verge surrounded it. They strolled leisurely around, Violet pushing Jean in the pram. The reservoir contained over two million gallons of water. There was a rain gauge set in the verge, surrounded by a short spiked cast iron fence, painted in the same waterworks green. Should the level of the water rise too much there was a cast iron overflow pipe. Copper wires were strung across the reservoir to stop birds settling in the water. There were two large copper mesh screens to filter out any foreign bodies. At the bottom of the reservoir were three long pipes which curved up and emerged above ground like three gigantic silver snakes that disappeared through the outside wall of the garden and which led into the lane. Fire tenders could draw off water from these pipes in case of fire. Near the entrance gates an eighty-foot-high cast iron twin standpipe stood majestically overlooking the whole property. A powerful engine pumped water up one side of the pipe and down the other to give enough pressure to serve the people of Devonport with clean drinking water.

Violet and John couldn't have been happier. 'We are going to be so happy here John, a detached cottage in its own grounds, it's wonderful.'

'We have certainly fallen on our feet,' he answered.

Chapter 6

John settled into his new job well and found that his duties were varied and many. He tested the water for purity, took rain gauge readings and managed the small chlorine plant. In addition he was also engaged in searching out leaks in the village of Stoke and the surrounding district. He became a familiar figure to the locals riding around on his single speed bicycle with his sounding stick and tools strapped to the crossbar. Violet was a full-time housewife, looking after baby Jean, keeping the cottage clean, as well as washing, ironing and cooking John's meals. She was soon able to use the sewing machine and taught herself to make clothes for Jean and turn collars for John. She spent hours on this machine.

'What are you making now Vi?'

'Just a summer frock for Jean. Do you like it?'

'It's lovely. You're very clever.'

'Oh, go on with you,' she smiled.

After a pause, he said 'I was thinking of getting a few chickens, so we could have our own eggs. What do you think?'

'Where would you keep them?' she asked.

'I could build a coop and run down at the bottom of the garden, just by the allotments. I'd only want half a dozen. We've got plenty of land.'

'I'd be happy, if you are.'

'That's settled then. I'll get some timber and a roll of netting wire and build one.'

'Jean and I can watch you build it.'

So John got to work and built a large coop with a run twenty yards long and two yards wide. He bought six young chickens from Mr Cundy who had the fields next to the reservoir. Violet liked this venture, especially the thought of collecting fresh eggs every day.

Since Jean had been born John spent more evenings at the pub enjoying his beer and the company of his friends. He often asked Violet to accompany him but she had no interest in going to the pub.

'Anyway, who would look after Jean?' she asked.

'Perhaps we could get a babysitter.'

'And we would have to pay. There's never enough money as it is. I'm finding it hard to manage.'

He replied gruffly, 'I work hard for my pay and you've never gone short.'

'It's just so hard to manage. That's all I'm saying.'

John was secretive about the wages he earned. Violet never made enquiries and accepted the amount that he gave her weekly. He always had enough money for his tobacco and beer. He was now smoking an ounce of Condor Three-Twist each week. There were three strands of tobacco which had to be cut off with a knife, rolled in the palm of the hand and then pushed into the pipe bowl. It would stink the house out.

Violet also noticed that her husband had a nasty trait she hadn't seen before, which she hated. Sometimes after coming home from the pub he would be very jovial, but at other times he would be morose and belligerent. It seemed that if he drank just that extra pint, it would turn his mood. And Violet disliked him intensely when he was like this, though she never said anything to antagonise him.

The chickens started laying and it was a joy to collect the eggs each day. John fed them on boiled potato peelings and any other scrap food there was. He used a large cast iron pot which he heated over the Primus stove. He also bought chicken feed from the local Co-op in Stoke village. Later he built a wooden workshop near where the chicken coop was and busied himself making shelves and cupboards, which added to or enhanced the furniture they had. Violet was so grateful and always praised him on his natural ability and skill.

But Violet was forced to scrimp and save as much as she could because John still expected a hot meal every day. She developed wonderful culinary skills and could rustle up mouth-watering dishes out of hardly anything. Her Cornish pasties were a speciality. The short crust pastry was made using a knife, not her hands, because, as she said, 'You have to keep the pastry cool.' The filling was made of skirt of beef, potato, onion and swede, and the pastry was hand crimped. The pasties were then cooked in the oven for an hour or so. They were John's favourite. He loved them.

Since living at the 'res', as the cottage became known, Violet had made friends with a woman of about the same age as herself. Her name was Rene Lamble and she lived with her husband Bert and her parents, fifty yards down the lane from the cottage. She was short and rotund and had problems with arthritis, which made her waddle like a duck. Rene and Violet became good friends and spent many an hour in each other's company, chatting over a cup of tea and home-baked buns.

Rene and Bert didn't have any children, and Rene, not being a good cook, bought her cakes and buns from Baskervilles, the local bakery.

'I wish I could cook like you do, Vi!' she exclaimed one day.

'I could always teach you, if you like,' replied Violet.

'Would you really? That's very kind of you.'

So Violet began teaching Rene to cook. But it was never successful, even with Violet looking over her shoulder and talking her through every step. Eventually, Rene became exasperated and gave up.

John, as well as doing his duties as reservoir keeper, was doing private plumbing jobs, such as repairing burst pipes. He had taught himself after watching plumbers at work. He did give some of this extra money to Violet, but kept the bulk for himself. His friends in the pub thought him a generous man as he was known to say to them, 'I'll get these, put your money away.' They didn't know he wasn't as generous to his family. Violet still loved him for all his faults, and at times he was tender towards her and Jean.

'I do love you Vi, you know that don't you?' he said after they had finished their meal one evening.

'Yes, and I love you too, but sometimes you can be quite horrible to me, especially when you've had too much beer.'

'I'll try to turn over a new leaf. I won't drink so much.'

'If only you could. That would make me happy.'

He really tried his best, but the call of the beer was too strong. Violet's family members came to see them from time to time but she never told them her troubles. Ivy knew what John was like when he had drunk too much because Jack would often join him in the Stoke Inn for a drink and had seen him in a belligerent mood.

John never missed work through drinking too much and, when he came home from work, he would make a fuss of Jean, bouncing her on his lap and singing songs, which made her laugh. One of his favourite songs was called the 'Five Fifteen':

The five fifteen, I hear the whistle blowing,
The five fifteen, my anchor's going slow,
The five fifteen, down the line we're running,
Bang go the gates for the five fifteen.

You leave your office at five o'clock,
Run to the butchers for your steak and chops,
Get an *Evening Herald* and a penny magazine,
And you run like hell for the five fifteen.

Living in the country far from town,
Trams and buses buzz around,
Living in a field where the grass grows green,
We run like hell for the five fifteen.

Mother's in her chair singing home sweet home,
Father's in his chair singing baritone.

When John came home from the pub feeling drunk he often forced himself upon his wife. She hated this sort of love-making, but gave in like the dutiful wife she was. She used a douche as a means of birth control, but the inevitable happened in May 1935.

'John, I'm pregnant again. But we can't afford another baby. It's hard enough with one.'

'Is there anything that you could take, to get rid of it?'

'I feel awful even thinking about doing something like that, but we can't afford to feed another mouth.'

'Is there anything you could take?'

'Someone told me that quinine might terminate a pregnancy, but where would I get it?'

'I'll ask around and see what I can do.'

He managed somehow to get hold of some. But it didn't work. And she felt so ashamed that she had even thought about doing something like that. So, during the summer of 1935, she was getting bigger and bigger. They were both resigned to the fact that they would have another mouth to feed and would just have to make the best of the situation. John's sister Lucy had agreed to stay at the 'res' to look after him and Jean when Violet had her confinement.

On 29 January 1936 at the Durnford Street Nursing Home, Stonehouse, after another hard and difficult labour, Mother gave birth to me. I weighed eight and a half pounds. Father was overjoyed when he saw me, with my shock of black hair and blue eyes. They had already selected my name, Anthony. 'He'll carry on the Trevail name, Vi!'.

Chapter 7

Jean was now four years old and I was one. We loved being around the chicken run; some of the original six had been replaced. Father had fixed up an electrical cable which ran underground from the cottage supply to his shed. He made an incubator for the chicks using a metal dustbin lid with a hole cut in the centre where he attached an electric light bulb. It worked really well and not many chicks were lost.

Life was rather repetitious for Mother. Monday was wash-day which took all day. Father had to be up early to light the copper in the wash house. He would fill it with water from the outside tap using a bucket. By the time Mother had made his breakfast of kippers on toast, followed by a mug of steaming tea – which he invariably poured into his saucer so as to blow on it to cool it down, before slurping it in huge gulps – the copper was well on its way to getting hot. Mother would then get Jean and me up, wash and dress us and feed us porridge, which had been soaking overnight to soften it up. I was then put in my pram. The water in the copper would be boiling by this time, so she could then add the Oxydol washing powder and begin the wash. Jean would play around as Mother fed the white cotton sheets and Father's white collarless work shirts into the water using a wooden poking stick. A wooden 'dolly' was used to mash the clothes around. Outside the stable door was a tap, under which she placed a metal bath. This was filled to the brim with water and a Reckitt's 'Blue Bag' was suspended from the tap by a piece of string so that it was submerged in the bath. This gave the sheets and shirts a brilliant white colour with a slightly blue tinge.

The washing took all day. The clothes had to be rinsed in the water then put through the hand-operated mangle so as to squeeze out as much water as possible and ease the drying process. Finally, the clothes were pegged out on the line. In summer, when the weather was good, they dried in no time at all, but in winter, when there was no 'dryth in the air', as Mother called it, she would hang them on a clothes horse in front of the coal fire. This filled the room with steam, made the windows run with condensation and the clothes smell of smoke.

* * *

On 26 September 1937 Mother gave birth to her second daughter, who was named Patricia. Father was overwhelmed with her and she became the apple of his eye. Shortly after this, he rented a Reddifusion wireless set and life took on a new meaning in the household. Mother loved to listen to the musical evenings and Father liked the boxing match commentaries as well as the music hall shows. Father was now only going to the pub a couple of evenings a week, though he had a habit of going out for a drink on Sunday before lunch, and on a few occasions came in late to find his meal dried up. He would be rather annoyed but managed to control his temper.

We were all growing up and Mother took us out most sunny days in summer, usually to Central Park where there was a boating pond and plenty of swings and roundabouts. Sometimes she took us to see the horses at the Vincents.

Father was very good at growing things in the garden and we were fortunate to have lots of land for vegetables. He planted shallots, potatoes, runner beans, broad beans, onions, beetroot and parsnips. Mother made wonderful soups and delicious roast dinners.

We were out of doors most days in summer. On particularly warm days, Mother bathed us in the wash house, in a tin bath, which was taken off the nail where it hung outside.

She took water from the copper, which had been lit earlier. Because she couldn't afford perfumed soap she made do by cutting slices from the unperfumed green Fairy soap. Father had made some holes in a discarded Tate and Lyle syrup tin to which he attached a piece of wire for a handle. Mother would agitate this tin in the hot water which produced lots of suds, ideal for bathing children.

So we all had a healthy colour and got on well with each other. We occupied Mother's attention most of the time and Jean's plaintive cries of 'I want … I want … I want…' were long forgotten as she came up to her fifth birthday. By now I was two and a half and Patricia, now shortened to Pat, was ten months old. The big day came for Jean to start school and, in September 1938, she was enrolled at Somerset Place School for Boys and Girls. Her teacher was Miss Kneebone whom she adored. Mr Glanville, the headmaster, was a wonderful caring man and worked hard for the welfare of his children. Jean loved school and every day Mother took Pat and me with Jean to the school and met her at the end of the day.

The year that Jean started school Mother and Father began discussing a man named Hitler. We were too young to understand what they were saying but sensed that all was not right by the worried look on Mother's face and the way that they would whisper when we were in hearing distance.

'That bleddy Hitler and his bleddy Nazi army have captured Austria, Vi!'

'Mind your language John. The children might hear.'

'I'm sorry, but he is a you-know-what.'

'I just don't like what's going on. Rene told me there might be another war.'

All through that summer there were more and more rumours, and Mother and Father were always glued to the wireless. On 15 September the British Prime Minister, Neville Chamberlain, met Adolf Hitler at the Berghof at Berchtesgaden to try to come up with a solution to avert war. At later meetings with Hitler it seemed that Chamberlain had succeeded and returned to a hero's welcome in London. The British people on the whole were disgusted by the antics of Hitler.

Father was asked to attend a meeting with the Chairman of the Water Committee, the city water engineer and other members to discuss air raid precautions. He was there because Rowdens Reservoir was featured in the minutes. The Chairman reported that the City Council saw war as a real threat and that they had to be ready, just in case. The water engineer read out what would need to be done at the 'res':

Shelter to be constructed in the earth bank, surrounding the reservoir, either timber or secured by reinforced concrete head and side trees. It will have a gas proof entrance. Accommodation for the reservoir keeper, and a family of four to five persons. Estimated cost £40. Adjoining this shelter would be another construction for an Air Raid Wardens post which would accommodate five to eight persons. Cost £70.

It was then that Father realised the threat that Hitler was posing. He didn't tell my mother too much because he knew that she would worry herself to death.

My sister Pat celebrated her first birthday on 26 September; Mother made her an iced cake with one candle on it. She also made cheese straws, butterfly buns, coconut pyramids and jelly to go with the pink blancmange rabbit made in a mould. The five of us had a party with games and finished off with a singsong. She had also boiled up some milk in a shallow pan and, when it cooled, scraped off the cream from the top, which we all loved.

The ominous threat of war overshadowed Christmas 1938 and Mother was getting more worried. Life carried on as usual and on 29 January 1939 I celebrated my third birthday. Mother made the same special effort and we all had a wonderful time. She had made me a chocolate cake with three candles on the top and the usual birthday fare. She was a wizard at making scrumptious food. Father sang some of his songs, one of which was this one:

There was a little man and he had a tin can,
And the beer he used to swallow,
Down by the canteen door,
The barmaid she would holler,
No beer today, no beer today, no beer today on Sunday,
Come again on Monday,
Goodbye beer forever ever more,
Your earthly days are nearly o'er,
And when you're dead and in your grave,
They'll tickle your feet for lemonade.

We all had a lovely time and were so happy. And then, on 31 March, Neville Chamberlain told a packed House of Commons that if Hitler invaded Poland, Britain would provide that country with military assistance. On 27 April conscription was introduced.

'Does that mean you'll have to join up John?' Mother asked.

'No, my job is classed as of national importance, so if there is a war and God forbid that it will come to that, I won't have to join up.'

'Thank goodness for that. I couldn't cope without you being here.'

'Anyway, let's not worry before we have to. The children will sense it and get upset. We won't talk about it in front of them.'

'Oh, please God don't let there be another war. Look what happened to my father in the last one.'

Father put his arms around her and she laid her head on his shoulder. 'Don't worry, everything will be all right.' But Mother wasn't convinced.

Plymouth City Council, anticipating war, asked for volunteers to be trained in civil defence. Father immediately volunteered to be an air raid precautions (ARP) warden, and was accepted. He started intensive training and he and his comrades had a good laugh at some of the antics they got up to. But behind the jovial banter many of the volunteers could see the ominous signs of war.

One day, when Father had just returned from ARP practice, Mother asked, 'I'm really worried John, do you think there will really be a war?'

'I doubt it. Hitler talks big. Someone ought to bump him off. I'd do it if I had a gun,' Father replied.

'Ivy said that Jack could be called up to serve the king.'

'Yes, he probably will have to enlist, because his job isn't classed as of national importance. I told you I won't be called up. I'll be here to take care of you and the children, so please don't worry yourself over anything.'

Mother felt comforted by his words, but they were not enough to dispel all her fears and worries.

The summer of 1939 was very warm and sunny and we spent a lot of time out of doors and were healthy and suntanned. Father forbade us to open the door to the path which led up to the 'res' because it was dangerous and if we fell into the water we would probably drown. We didn't disobey him, and because the days were long and light we used to play at the front of the cottage where Mother and Father would sit on a wooden form enjoying the sun. Father lit his pipe and I enjoyed the smell of the tobacco mixed with the wonderful fragrance of the honeysuckle tree, which grew against the reservoir wall, that wafted in the cool evening air.

Father had built another chicken run which I had helped him with. I also helped to feed the chickens. I always had to assist Father when he was doing a project. I didn't always enjoy it because sometimes I wanted to play instead.

'Tony, if you don't behave yourself and do as I say, I'll put you in a cooked meat shop with a muzzle on.'

I didn't understand what he meant, but it sounded awful to my young ears and working with him was better, so I yielded under the threat.

But these tranquil times were to be the last for a very long time. In August Mother was pregnant again, for my parents didn't use any form of contraception. It was still warm at the beginning of September, and on Sunday the third Mother was preparing the dinner and listening to the wireless. Father was in the pub. We children were in the sitting room. The church service being broadcast was interrupted for a special announcement. The announcer introduced the prime minister, and Mother knew in her heart what he was about to say. Her whole being tingled and her head was a little fuzzy as a shiver ran up her spine. She heard the words, 'Britain is now at war with Germany.' She felt a sharp pain in her hand; unknowingly she had bitten it so hard that she had drawn blood.

'What will happen to us all now?' she cried.

We stopped playing when we heard Mother crying. We looked at her in wide-eyed astonishment. We had never seen her cry before. She herded us back into the sitting room and put her arms around us, tears still trickling down her pale cheeks, my sister Jean trying to wipe them away with her pinafore as well as the blood on her hand.

'What is the matter? Please don't cry mum,' she said.

I was really upset and started to blub. 'What's Mother crying for?'

Much too young to understand the severity of the news that Mother had just heard, Pat just squirmed and gurgled.

Father had been enjoying a pint at the Stoke Inn when he and his mates heard the news. He gulped it down and quickly made for home knowing that Mother would be upset. He rushed in the door and hugged everyone.

'Oh John. I'm so afraid. It's dreadful news.'

'Shush, nothing will happen to any of us, I promise.'

Father had said the first thing that came into his head to comfort Mother. She felt a little better after what he had said, and although the Sunday roast smelled delicious, she had lost her appetite.

The terrible thought of war was on everyone's minds, especially as only twenty-two years before granddad Ruthven had had his legs blown off. Most people of my parents' age had relatives that had been killed or wounded in the First

World War. The present threat of another war brought back horrendous memories.

Uncle Jack received his call-up papers and was conscripted into the Devon Regiment of the army. Auntie Ivy was in tears, although they both knew that it was inevitable. He was told to report to Colchester for basic training in a week's time. Uncle Jack, Auntie Ivy, Mother and Father arranged to spend an evening together before Jack departed. Mother's friend Rene, who lived down the lane from the cottage, agreed to look after us children. They went to a pub called The Mount Pleasant for sandwiches and drinks. Jack wasn't his usual confident and brash self and the others tried their best to cheer him up. Auntie Ivy was tearful all evening and kept breaking down. Father suggested that they return to the 'res' for a cup of coffee. He was 'tiddly' and in good spirits. Mother only had one shandy. When they arrived at the cottage Rene had the fire stoked up and blazing. Father thanked her and walked her home, which only took five minutes or so. When he returned Mother had boiled the kettle and the smell of Camp Coffee greeted his nostrils. They talked till well past midnight.

Jack said to Mother and Father, 'Promise to take care of Ivy for me when I'm away.'

Ivy said, 'Of course they will darling.'

'Promise Vi. Promise me John.'

Mother and Father promised to do what he had asked then they all hugged and kissed.

'We'll see you off at the station, Jack,' Father said.

'I'd like that very much,' Jack replied.

Soon after they left, Father and Mother went to bed. Father was snoring within five minutes but Mother could not sleep; her head was filled with disturbing thoughts.

* * *

A week later we all accompanied Uncle Jack to North Road Station to say goodbye. The platform was full of people. Many of the men looked like they were conscripts as they were carrying small suitcases. We heard the train whistle as it came into sight. The clanking beast had steamed up from Cornwall and was approaching Platform 7. As it chugged by we all got covered in black smuts from the thick smoke pouring out of the funnel. Auntie Ivy was sobbing uncontrollably as Uncle Jack put his arms around her and tried to console her. We children wondered what was going on; then Jean started to cry, which set me off.

'Why is Auntie Ivy crying?' asked Jean.

Mother lifted her up and said, 'There, there, don't cry. Uncle Jack is going away for a while and Auntie Ivy is feeling very sad.'

'I don't want him to go away. Why can't he stay?' Her cheeks were wet from the tears and she had two 'candles' dripping from her nose which ran onto her lips. Mother wiped them away with a handkerchief.

Uncle Jack was kissing Auntie Ivy. 'Don't cry Ivy, everything will be all right, just you wait and see.'

'Oh darling, please take care.' Her mascara had run down her face and had left smudges on Jack's face as well.

'Of course I'll take care, you know me.'

'Yes I do know you and that's what I'm afraid of.' He could feel a hard lump inside his throat, and his temples were throbbing.

The train came to a halt with a loud screech of brakes. The carriage doors were flung open and passengers streamed off. Father shook Jack's hand and said, 'Best of luck Jack, take care of yourself, keep your nose clean and you'll survive. Please write mate.'

'I will John.'

But I was getting fed up with all of this and wanted to see the train more closely. 'Want to see puff puff,' I said, pulling Mother's hand towards the engine.

'Keep still Tony and stop pulling your mother,' said Father, giving me a look that made me hide behind Mother's coat. I was afraid of him when he gave me that nasty look.

Uncle Jack found a seat in the third-class compartment, put his small case on the overhead luggage rack and came back to the door, which was now closed. He lowered the leather strap to let the window down and leaned out.

'The train standing on Platform 7 is the 3.55 to Paddington, calling at all principal stations. Please close all doors and stand well clear.'

The guard blew his whistle and waved his little green flag and smartly jumped aboard. The engine burst into life with a toot on the whistle, the wheels sent up showers of sparks as they spun round on the rails, and black smoke belched out of the funnel, once more covering the people on the platform with soot. There were shouts of 'Cheerio', 'Good luck' and 'Write soon'. Steam filled the air as the train started to rumble past.

Ivy clung to Jack's hand as the train moved slowly forwards and began to gather speed. People were running down the platform trying to keep up with the train. Ivy shouted, 'Write soon darling, I love you.'

'As soon as I can I will darling. And I love you too. Now let go of my hand.'

But Ivy held on to Jack's hand too long. Her eyes were misty with tears, and she didn't see the raised flagstone. Down she went, knocking the breath out of her lungs.

'Ivy!' Jacked yelled back.

She had grazed her hands and torn two large holes in the knees of her stockings. The pain made her cry even more, and the mascara ran down her cheeks like ugly black tramlines. Through her tears she could see Jack's white face hanging out of the window. Then the back end of the train disappeared into the tunnel. Father was first on the scene and helped her to a bench.

'There, there, take is easy,' he said.

'What happened?' she gasped.

'You've winded yourself; you'll be all right in a minute.'

A lump began to grow visibly on her forehead. We were all stood around her. But she recovered very quickly and soon became very embarrassed at the thought of the spectacle she must have made. ‘Did anybody see me?’

‘No, nobody was looking,’ Father replied, a solemn look on his face.

He handed her his handkerchief; but inside he was laughing, and to the discerning eye his rotund belly was shaking like a blancmange that had just been relieved of its mould.

Chapter 8

Jack made his way back to the compartment and sat down by the window. Opposite him was a man of about the same age as himself and a woman with two children of about twelve or thirteen, a boy and a girl. Beside him was a middle-aged man with a woman who seemed to be his wife and beside them an old man sucking on an unlit pipe. The man opposite took out a packet of Player's cigarettes, put one in his mouth and proffered the packet towards Jack.

'Fag mate? My father gave me these as a going away present.'

'Ta very much, I'm sure,' Jack said appreciatively.

Jack flicked up the top of his Ronson petrol lighter, spun the milled wheel and the flame sprung into life. They both lit up and blew out the cool blue smoke. Jack wasn't used to smoking these expensive cigarettes but always enjoyed the experience when he had the chance.

'How far are you going?' The man had a very strong Cornish accent, which was much different to Jack's Devon burr.

'I've been called up and I'm on my way to join the army.'

'Well blow me down, so am I.'

'What regiment?' they both asked in unison.

Jack spoke first, 'The Devons. What else, seeing as how I live here? Mind you I'd rather not be joining any regiment at all, but who's got a choice with this bleddy lunatic, Hitler?'

'Put it there boy, so am I.' He took Jack's hand and shook it vigorously. Jack started to feel a little better.

'I'm Archibald Penfold and I come from Looe; everyone calls me Archie.'

'I'm Jack Lambert.'

Archie told Jack that he was single and that the men in his family were fishermen and had been for generations. They both talked about their respective families and showed each other the photographs they had brought. Jack showed him a photo of Ivy. 'This is my lovely wife Ivy.'

Archie stared at the photo and said, 'I saw her at the station with you and some other people. She's a real smasher; you're a very lucky bloke. I hope she didn't hurt herself too much when she fell on the platform!'

Everyone in the compartment was friendly and shared sandwiches and flasks of tea with each other. The time flew by and after five and a half hours the train rumbled into Paddington Station.

'This is the first time I've been to London. How about you Jack?'

'First time for me too. Apparently we have to go on the Underground to Liverpool Street Station.'

Archie said, 'I haven't got a clue as to where to go.'

'Let's ask someone,' Jack said. He spied a porter laden down with luggage. 'Excuse me mate, can you tell us how to get to Liverpool Street Station?'

'Yus mite. Follow the signs to the Underground and jump on the Circle Line, that'll tike you.'

After thanking him they lugged their suitcases to the Underground. It was cold and draughty and had an unusual smell. The platform was packed with people. Soon afterwards a train appeared out of a tunnel before slowing rapidly to a screeching halt. The doors opened and people streamed out. At the same time, the people on the platform rushed at the doors.

'Come on Archie, when in Rome.'

'What do you mean?'

'Let's get on.'

They pushed their way onto the train, but it was packed and they had to stand all the way to Liverpool Street.

'Phew! That was an experience, wasn't it?' asked Jack.

At Liverpool Street Station they boarded another train, this time bound for Colchester. On arrival in that town they were directed to a large lorry containing other men that was waiting to transport them to the 99th Primary Training Centre. They arrived at the camp gate at ten o'clock. Two drill instructors were waiting for them, brandishing wooden canes which they beat on the side of the lorry as it rolled slowly to a halt on the parade ground. They were shouting obscenities at the raw recruits to get out and fell in.

'Right you 'orrible lot, get out! Get out! Get out! Move it!' The terrified new recruits scrambled over each other in their rush to get out of the back of the lorry.

'Listen carefully. When I call out your name, you will answer "Present corporal." Have you got it?'

There was no answer. 'Have you got it?' he yelled.

'Yes corporal!' they all shouted.

'I want you to pick up your luggage and, when I say "At the double", follow me. Do you understand?'

'Yes corporal!'

'At the double!'

The corporal took off at a run and the men ran as best as they could after him, lugging their suitcases. After a few hundred yards he came to a stop by a low building.

'This is your barrack room, B6,' he said, pointing to a painted sign on the door. 'When you get inside, pick a bed, drop your suitcases and parade outside in two minutes.'

Everyone rushed into the barrack room, falling over each other in their panic to find a bed, before going back outside. They were marched, in a ragged fashion, to the cookhouse for a supper of egg and beans on toast, and a mug of undrinkable tea. Not much later they returned to the barrack room.

It seemed that no sooner had their heads touched the pillow than they were awoken by the piercing bugle call of reveille from the parade ground. An angry corporal marched into the barrack room hitting each bed with a short stick and shouting at the top of his voice for everybody to be up, washed, shaved and outside in ten minutes. No one knew what had hit them and there was a mad rush to get to the wash rooms. There was only cold water for shaving. In the panic, Jack cut himself with his razor (which he hardly ever done before).

'What have we let ourselves in for Archie?'

But Archie just grunted.

'Outside! Outside! Outside!' The corporal was relentless in his mission, expostulating with anyone who got in his way.

'Fall in, in three ranks! Come on, at the double!'

There was mayhem. Men were falling over each other as they sought to form three ranks. There was a hubbub of voices.

'Be quiet you nincompoops!' the corporal yelled. Silence fell.

They were marched to the cookhouse for breakfast, which consisted of 'slices of porridge', a fried egg, fried bread and a mug of tea.

Over the next week they were issued with all the equipment that a fighting soldier would need. Uniforms were issued; a Lee–Enfield .303 rifle and bayonet were signed for. They were all given eating irons, a billy can, a water bottle, army issue underwear, boots, gaiters, a green Blanco kit for the webbing, black boot polish, a kit bag and finally a 'housewife' (a small cloth packet containing needles, cotton and wool for darning socks). They were instructed on how to make a bed pack, how to 'bull' boots with spit and polish until you could see your face in them, and how to use a gas mask.

In the second week the training began in earnest. Now they were up at six a.m., changing into PE kit before running five miles before breakfast. At first, every new recruit found this devastating, but soon it became exhilarating and all without exception felt the fittest that they had ever been. Jack had been very fit when he was doing boxing training but this was something else.

All the food that was given them in the cookhouse was eaten ravenously, even though the quality left a lot to be desired. Every task was done 'at the double'. Every day they had marching and rifle drill. Sergeant McPherson, a Scotsman, took over from the corporal and put them through their paces.

'A-a-attention! Stand at e-e-ease! A-a-attention! Stand at e-e-ease! By the left, in columns of three, quick march! Halt! Stand still you 'orrible lot!'

Jack was beginning to enjoy the experience, as did Archie. March, march, march in the mornings with a short break if the sergeant thought they had worked hard enough. The Salvation Army, The 'Sally Ann', came around in a van with tea and buns, which could be bought by the soldiers.

'Slo-o-ope arms! Order arms! Pre-e-esent arms!'

As they carried out these movements they all shouted as one, 'Up two three, over two three, down two three.' It was exhausting work, but doing it over and over again they came to do it in unison.

Living so close together, all day every day, tempers became frayed, and many were on a short fuse. The barrack room was cleaned up and tidied every day; room orderlies were appointed to make sure that everyone did his share of the work. Sergeant McPherson inspected their kit every day and woe betide anyone who was not up to scratch. The miscreant would be made to run around the parade ground with his rifle above his head until his arms felt like dropping off.

Their rifles had to be cleaned daily and their bayonets sharpened to a razor's edge with a whetstone until it could 'split a human hair down the middle', according to the sergeant. When they engaged in bayonet practice, straw filled sandbags were positioned with a rope tied at the top and the bottom secured to a wooden frame. A sandbag represented the enemy. They lined up in three columns.

'Right you lot, fix bayonets!' They fixed their bayonets to the muzzles of their rifles and awaited instructions. 'Listen carefully. You run at the enemy screaming your bloody heads off. That puts the wind up the blighter. Then you thrust your bayonet through him and twist it to pull it out. Then go on to the next enemy. Now, let's hear those blood curdling screams.'

The men let out the most hideous screams. They became quite hysterical doing it.

'This is serious,' said Sergeant McPherson. 'It might save your life before very long.'

The men really enjoyed the bayonet practice, but they also saw the solemn side to it. All, as one man, despised Sergeant McPherson, but nevertheless they were in awe of him. When he walked into the barrack room, the first person to see him shouted out, 'NCO present!' Immediately everyone stopped what they were doing and stood at the bottom of their beds to attention. They would always be on tenterhooks because he usually found something that wasn't to his satisfaction. He wore white gloves to see whether there was any dust on their locker tops. If he did find something the culprit would have to cut the grass verge with a pair of scissors, or paint coal with white wash using a toothbrush.

The men soon came up to standard. There were a few who would never make good soldiers because of their naturally poor physique or aptitude. One such was an Irish boy named McCurry who came from a small village in Ireland and spoke with a terrible stammer. He was very timid and had been victimised by a bully named Grainger. He was also terrified of the sergeant. Jack and Archie had befriended him and took him under their wings. Jack hated bullies.

There were comedians too, and one especially was Slim Atkins who suffered greatly with flatulence, but who kept the men in stitches. One of his favourite acts was to wait until the barrack lights were out and in the darkness whisper, 'Quick lads, I've got one coming.' Everyone looked in the direction of his bed in the darkness. He would lay on top of his bed on his back with his legs pulled back on his chest. With a lighted match in front of his bottom, he would ignite the extruded gas which flashed green and lit up the whole barrack room. All the men roared their heads off. Invariably the sergeant would storm in. 'What's going on in here? Get to sleep you stupid Jessies. If there's any more of it, I'll have you outside on the parade ground.' They had to push their faces into their pillows to stifle their laughter.

After one particularly strenuous day McCurry had gone to bed early, utterly exhausted and soon after fell into a deep sleep. Grainger and a couple of his cronies were whispering together and looking towards the recumbent McCurry. Archie came across to Jack. 'They are up to something, better keep an eye on them.'

'I was just thinking that,' replied Jack.

Grainger and his cronies crept towards McCurry and when their heads were only inches from his head shouted at the top of their voices as one, 'NCO present!'

McCurry sat bolt upright to attention, his eyes like saucers and shaking like a leaf. There was a silence before he whined quietly at them, 'Now look what you've done. You've made me pee the bed.'

Grainger stifled a laugh and bawled, 'You dirty swine!. Hey! McCurry has piddled the bed.'

The three of them roared with laughter. But Jack saw red and launched himself at Grainger, shouting, 'What did you do that for?'

'What's it to you? Keep your nose out if you know what's good for you.'

Grainger side stepped, and punched Jack in the solar plexus. Jack fell to the floor, winded. Archie had followed Jack and was grappling with the other two. One of the men held Archie while the other one landed him a blow to the side of the head. Archie crumpled. The rest of the men in the billet shouted out, 'Come on, fight fair.'

Jack saw Grainger's foot coming towards his head and rolled out of the way at the same time catching Grainger's foot and twisting it, bringing him crashing down, catching his head a glancing blow on McCurry's iron bedstead. Blood poured from the wound. Grainger howled. Jack jumped on his chest and, pinning his arms with his knees, punched him on the nose, splitting and crushing the bone, which made a sound like a ripe tomato hitting a brick wall. More blood spurted and he pleaded, 'Don't hit me again, I've had enough.'

Archie meanwhile was being pummelled by the other two. Jack now turned his attention to these and, with a final kick at Grainger's body, attacked one of them, grabbing him around the neck and pulling him off Archie. Archie then punched him senseless and turned to help Jack. Archie already had a fine physique acquired from his time as a fisherman hauling in nets. But Jack's opponent had already given up. All five of them were bruised and bloodied and Grainger had to report to the sick bay for treatment. (He told the medical officer that he had fallen against the cast iron stove in the barrack room, for which Jack was grateful.) The others cleaned up in the wash-room. No one was picked on again after that and McCurry was eternally grateful to Jack and Archie. Everyone eventually got to bed with the acrid smell of McCurry's urine-soaked blanket drying near the stove. After that incident McCurry began to change and army life toughened him up.

* * *

One day they were on the firing ranges and Jack found that he was becoming a crack shot.

'Keep that up Lambert and you will make a marksman.'

'Thanks Sergeant.'

McCurry overheard two corporals talking in which it became clear that marksmen would end up as snipers. He told Jack what he had heard. Jack's shooting skill subsequently diminished.

'What's wrong with you Lambert? You couldn't hit a barn at twenty yards.'

'My eyes seem to blur up when I'm concentrating on the target, Sarge.'

'Report to the MO then and get an eye test.'

The MO couldn't find much wrong with his eyes, even though Jack misread some of the letters. 'Are you trying to work your ticket son?' the officer asked.

'Certainly not, sir,' Jack replied.

'Very well, I'll make out my report,' he said, with a twinkle in his eyes.

Jack never found out what was in the report, but his aim remained poor and Sergeant McPherson never mentioned it again.

The training was very tough but they *were* being turned into fighting machines. Arms drill was the hardest and to drop your rifle was a cardinal sin. Archie wasn't the best and one day he dropped his rifle whilst presenting arms.

'What are you doing, you Cornish pasty?'

'My gun slipped out my hand Sergeant, I'm sweating so much.'

'You dropped your what?' screamed the sergeant, two inches away from Archie's face. Archie smelt his hot rancid breath on his face and his stomach heaved.

'My rifle, sarge,' he stammered.

Sergeant McPherson grabbed his crotch with his left hand and held Archie's rifle with his right hand. 'This is my rifle and this is my gun. This one's for fighting and this one's for fun. Have you got it?'

'Yes Sergeant.'

'Well don't forget it. Now double around the parade ground with it above your head until I tell you to stop.'

Archie ran with the rifle above his head. It started to rain. Two hours later he was still running, absolutely done in. He was then told to stop. He collapsed and was taken to the sick bay.

Everyone was missing home and letters arrived now and then. The letters they sent back were censored. Jack had received a couple from Ivy. Archie's mother wrote to him; he missed her terribly. Many of the soldiers were very homesick and wept quietly when they were in their beds at night. They were told that bromide was added to their tea to suppress their sexual urges. They believed this to be true, though at the end of each day they were too exhausted from the strict regime to have any sexual thoughts.

Their training was coming to an end and they had been told that they would get a seventy-two-hour leave pass on completion, before their posting. Archie hadn't been feeling well since his rifle punishment and had stayed in the sick bay for a couple of days. He was still feeling nauseous and light headed. Jack advised him to report in sick again, but he didn't want to miss the passing out parade. They were rehearsing very hard for this parade, as it was only two weeks away. They had just carried out a particular drill and were stood at ease while Sergeant McPherson walked through the ranks to do a mock inspection. He stood behind one soldier and bawled in his ear, 'Am I hurting you laddie?'

'No Sergeant,' came the reply.

'Well I should be. I'm standing on your hair. Now get it cut you scruffy individual.'

'Yes Sarge.' His hair was already short, but not apparently short enough. A few men sniggered.

'I'll have the lot of you doubling round the square if you can't control yourselves, you bunch of Jessies.'

They went silent. Their hatred of the sergeant had turned to one of respect as they discerned that he had a heart of gold under his brittle exterior.

But Archie wasn't feeling at all well and felt light headed as they stood there on parade. His legs felt like jelly and began to shake. He started to fall to the left. The soldier on his left instinctively moved to catch him but his bayonet went into Archie's neck and came out the other side, severing his carotid artery. Blood shot out and sprayed over the soldiers around him. He crashed to the ground.

Jack screamed out, 'Archie!'

Some panicked but Jack rushed to Archie and removed the rifle from the bayonet. 'Do something Sarge.' Sergeant McPherson rushed over and told Jack to pick up Archie's legs while he grabbed him under his arms. They rushed him to the sick bay. Archie's eyes were rolling and horrible gurgling sounds came from his throat. He left a trail of blood across the parade ground, the bayonet bobbing in his neck.

As they got to the sick bay Archie stopped making a noise. Jack knew that his best mate was dead.

Everyone was shaken up and dismissed for the rest of that day. A week later Archie's body was taken back to Looe and he was given a burial with full military honours. Jack, McCurry, Grainger, Atkins, Sergeant McPherson and the soldier whose bayonet had caused his death were the pall-bearers. After the funeral Jack spent some time talking to Mrs Penfold trying to comfort her about her loss; but she was inconsolable.

A week later, Jack's platoon passed out as the best all-round platoon. They all said that it was for Archie. They were all given seventy-two hours leave and Jack went home to Ivy in Plymouth.

Ivy was waiting for Jack as the train drew into the station. He was leaning out of the door and saw her almost immediately. 'Ivy,' he shouted.

'Jack, darling.' She fell into his arms and they kissed passionately.

Arm in arm they went home to their flat. Their lovemaking that night was wonderful. Ivy told him that she loved him so much. He got the bike out the next day and they spent a lovely time on the beach at Whitsand Bay in Cornwall. The sea was turbulent but they found a deep pool in which to swim. Then they laid themselves out on the warm sand, holding each other. He told her about his experiences and how sad he was at losing his friend Archie.

They had a wonderful weekend, and Violet and John invited them to their house for Sunday lunch, before he had to catch the train back and report for duty. But it was all too short and the tears flowed again.

'I don't know when I'll see you again Jack,' she said through her tears. 'Hopefully it won't be too long.'

But he didn't yet know where he would be posted.

Chapter 9

On 12 April 1940, Mother gave birth to her second son; he was christened John Sylvanus, his second name coming from the famous Cornish architect, an ancestor of the Trevails. He was a bonny baby with blond hair and blue eyes. I was now four and a bit, Jean was six and a half and Pat was three. Father had fitted up the other bedroom with two beds. I slept in one and Jean and Pat slept in the other.

Later that month some corporation workmen came to make a start on the air raid shelters and the wardens' post. They took ten weeks to finish them and during that time word had got about that they were being built and people in the district came to watch the progress. Many local people were building their own Anderson shelters in their back gardens for which they had to pay £8 for the privilege. Not many really thought that a few pieces of corrugated metal would be much of a deterrent against bombs, but they were to prove invaluable when the time came.

When the construction was complete Mother, Father and we children were very interested in our own shelter and went inside, shutting the heavy concrete gas-proof door which made a strange hollow sound when it closed. It also had an unusual smell. Father started to make sketches for the furniture that would be needed in it.

'We'll have four bunk beds; one for Jean, Tony and Pat, the other one for you Vi. Baby John will be in a crib. I'll build a little cupboard for a few necessities like candles and water and so on. So we should be quite comfy. That's if we ever have to use it.'

'Well I hope it doesn't come to that,' Mother said. 'I don't really like it, it's claustrophobic, and it has a strange smell, which I don't particularly like.'

We were happy that we were going to have our own bunk beds. 'I want to have a top one,' I pleaded.

'I'll see,' father replied.

He managed to acquire some timber from a friend of his and built the bunk beds. They were rectangular – five-foot long and two-foot wide, though Mother's was a little longer. Father nailed some strong woven material to the edges so that it sagged like a hammock. He made strong wooden brackets screwed into the concrete to support the bunks. I was given the top bunk on the right-hand side, which really pleased me. He had also made a little wooden ladder for me to climb up. He then built some wooden shelves and said to Mother, 'You'll have to stock up on tins of soup, in case we have to stay here for any length of time.'

'And where do you think the money is coming from to do that? I can hardly manage as it is.'

'I give you housekeeping every week, don't I?'

'Yes, but it's hard to make it stretch.'

'I can't give you any more, so you'll have to manage.'

'If you cut down on your pipe and drinking, I could do so much more.'

'I don't want to discuss it anymore and that's an end to it.'

Father managed to get hold of a paraffin heater-cum-stove so that Mother would be able to heat up soup and make simple meals in case we had to stay there for any length of time. In the domed ceiling of the shelter were two hollow, metal, fresh-air vents which protruded out onto the grass verge of the reservoir above; they had conical caps on the top to stop rain coming in. Father also constructed a wooden shed around both the shelters with a door at each end and one in the middle. The middle door led out to a path and the back lane. The ARP shelter had a telephone installed. I thought it was a wonderful place.

One day, Jean, Pat and I were playing in our shelter and Jean pulled the door from the inside, but she couldn't open it. It was pitch dark because Father hadn't installed an electric light. We were terrified and started to yell and cry. 'Mother! Help! We're locked in the shelter and can't get out.'

Fortunately Mother heard our muffled cries emanating from the air vents and came running to let us out. We rushed into her arms sobbing our hearts out. Father told us that the shelter was out of bounds for playing in and he put a padlock on the door.

Mother managed to get some blackout material which was used to cover all the windows of the cottage. There was not to be any light showing, which might help the German aeroplanes to see where to drop their bombs.

In the first few months of 1940 nothing much was happening and the 'phoney war' in Europe seemed such a long way off that many people were becoming complacent. Mother was feeling a little happier and asked Father if the German aeroplanes could reach Plymouth. 'They could, but I don't think that they will,' he told her. But she didn't ask him what he based this assumption on.

Auntie Ivy and her friend Ruby had left the sweet factory and were working in the Dockyard as capstan lathe operators at one end of the heavy turnery shop located in North Yard. Uncle Jack was still in England, but was moving around quite a bit. He had joined the Devons, but was permanently attached to the 18th Welsh regiment. Their letters were full of love for each other and they wrote every week. Auntie Ivy came to see us two or three times each week.

In May news came trickling through via the wireless and the *Western Morning News* that the British Expeditionary Force (BEF) in France was taking a beating from the Germans. The ports of Calais and Boulogne could not be used for supplying the BEF troops and a quarter of a million men were living on half-rations. The BEF together with the Belgians and the French were surrounded on three sides, their backs to the English Channel. On the beaches at Dunkirk the men found what shelter they could by digging holes in the sand to escape the screaming German Stukas which bombed them and the Messerschmitt 109Es which strafed the beach with their 20 mm cannons. Mother became very tense and agitated at the news and had visions of Adolf Hitler invading England. Father was more disappointed than worried.

'It's not over yet by a long chalk and, anyway, we've got right on our side,' he said.

'I couldn't bear it if the Germans came here. It would be better if we were all dead. I just worry about what might become of the children.'

'Don't talk daft Vi. It just won't happen. And don't say anything in front of the children; you'll put the wind up them good and proper.'

On 25 May, 5,000 British and French troops were captured. Eight or nine German armoured divisions surrounded the BEF and the allies, but because of the marshy conditions and the possibility of getting bogged down and becoming sitting ducks from air attack they stopped advancing. This turned out to be a partial salvation for the BEF. The next evening Operation Dynamo was put into action, the key objective being to rescue as many men and equipment as possible from Dunkirk. Vice Admiral Ramsay of Dover and his Chief of Staff Captain Day drew up a plan to use as many ships and boats to cross the channel for the evacuation. French warships, merchant vessels and a vast flotilla of sea-going craft, from paddle steamers to private small boats numbering 861, rescued over 886,000 British and allied troops. Of these vessels 243 were sunk and many lost their lives. It was aptly named the 'Miracle of Dunkirk'.

Many of the rescued men were brought to Millbay Docks in the Port of Plymouth before they rejoined their regiments or other organisations. The docks were filled with battle worn and injured men. The people of Plymouth turned out to greet them with tea and sandwiches and to thank them for their heroic efforts. The feelings of all were running high and many people were brought to tears by the sights that they saw. Mother had made a dozen pasties and wrapped them in towels to keep them hot and went with Father to greet them. In less than a minute the pasties had disappeared.

'Thanks missus. Bloomin' delicious!' a young soldier exclaimed.

'You're more than welcome. And thanks for all you've done for us.'

Mother and Father walked home, arms around each other, feeling that they had helped the war effort a little bit. We were all ears when they arrived home and they relayed the events to us.

Because of the heavy losses incurred by the BEF, an imminent invasion was expected. On 6 July 1940 we children were playing happily in front of the cottage. John was in his pram and it was a glorious warm sunny day. Mother was preparing the midday meal and listening to the wireless, singing along to Evelyn Laye's 'Let the People Sing'. Father was on his way home from a job that he had been doing. Then, the wailing of the air-raid warning siren rent the air and drowned out the summer sounds. We didn't take any notice because we had heard it so many times before when there had been a practice. But Mother stopped what she was doing and rushed outside, panic in her voice, 'Quick children, go to the shelter.' She picked the sleeping John out of his pram and quickly ushered us towards the shelter, which was about seventy yards from the cottage. As we ran we heard the noise of an aeroplane in the distance. When we reached the shelter we couldn't get in because of the padlock on the door. 'Children, go to the wardens' post.' That door too was locked.

By now Mother was frantic, and seeing her panic and distress we all started to cry. Then we heard the sound of guns going off somewhere in the city. 'Right,' she screamed. 'All of you get in the chicken coop!' She opened the door to the raucous squawks of the six residents who scrambled into the run, feathers flying everywhere. She pushed the three of us in and followed, with John still asleep in her arms. We sat on the floor in the droppings and feathers. Mother put her arms around us, like a mother hen, and said, 'Put your fingers in your ears.' We did as we were told because we were all terrified. Then we started to hear loud bangs. The aeroplane had an unusual-sounding engine noise, different to any that we had heard before.

A single German plane had dropped a bomb on a housing estate in the Swilly area, which was quite near where we lived. Three people were killed and six injured. Father had heard the siren go off as he was returning home and, as he was just passing Jean's school, ran into the shelter in Bunkers Hill. When he heard the exploding bombs he was worried about our safety, so he ran out and got on his bike and pedalled furiously, knowing that we were all at home. He realised that the shelter was still locked and that we wouldn't be in it.

By now the explosions had stopped and the aeroplane had disappeared into the distance. As he reached the cottage he dropped his bike and shouted out Mother's name as loud as he could. The 'all clear' siren was sounding now. 'Vi, where are you? Are you all all right?'

There was no answer from the cottage. We all heard Father's booming voice calling out to us.

We all shouted, 'Father! We're in the chicken coop!'

Father ran as fast as he could and, opening the door, saw us all cowering on the floor covered in feathers and bird droppings and smelling awful. 'What are you doing in there?'

'The shelter door was locked and so was the wardens' post. We had to get shelter somewhere,' declared Mother.

As we climbed out Father's faced creased into a wide smile, then his stomach began to shake. He couldn't control himself any longer and started to laugh, pointing to Mother's skirt which was covered in feathers and chicken droppings. 'You all smell awful,' he said, his florid face redder than ever and tears coming down his face. We children started to giggle at Father's antics.

'It's not funny. We were terrified,' wailed Mother, not at all amused.

'You would have been safer if you'd gone under the stairs,' he said.

'There's no room under the stairs. How could we? I just panicked. Fancy locking the shelter.'

'I won't lock it again,' he said.

Then she saw the funny side of it and we all laughed as we made our way to the cottage for a good wash and change of clothes. Baby John woke up when we got indoors. But Mother was very upset by this bombing raid and couldn't get it out of her mind.

The next day Father went to look at the damage the bombs had made and when he came home he gave me some small pieces of metal which had sharp edges. 'These are pieces of one of the bombs,' he said. It was the first of many pieces of shrapnel that I collected and it was used to barter for all sorts of things.

This had been the first bombing raid over city and marked the start of the Plymouth Blitz. Before the war was over, there would be another fifty-eight air raids with devastating effects.

The next day, Sunday, was a bright sunny day. Mother was busy cooking. At noon we had a lunch of belly pork, roast potatoes, carrots, peas and Yorkshire pudding, followed by semolina. At five o'clock we ate a 'top and bottom pie' (sometimes called a 'pasty pie') followed by egg custard tart and coconut pyramids. Father still poured his tea into his saucer and blew on it to cool it down before slurping it up. We all had to give thanks to God after every meal before we were allowed to leave the table: 'Thank the Lord for our tea. Amen. Please can we leave the table?'

'Yes you can,' replied Father.

'Can we play in the front, please?'

'Yes all right, but don't go out into the lane.'

Jean, Pat and myself were playing hopscotch. We had only been out for five minutes when the air-raid siren sounded across the city. We didn't have to be told what to do now and I ran as fast as I could to the shelter with my two sisters behind me. Father, Mother and baby John came in right after us. Father pushed us inside and said, 'Stay in there and don't come out under any circumstances. I'm off to the wardens' post to await orders.'

'Try not to be gone long, John,' Mother pleaded.

'I'll be back as soon as I can,' he replied as he rushed off.

We thought that Father was very brave.

This raid consisted of one bomber coming over the city. Bombs fell on South Milton Street, Cattedown. Some houses were demolished and more people lost their lives. Mother became very nervous and found it difficult to sleep at night. Father was on fire watch nearly every night now and spent his evenings in the wardens' post, which was furnished with a table and chairs, a blackboard, a telephone and a few comfortable armchairs that the wardens would use to catch some sleep if it were possible. Father found it difficult to go to the pub, because of his night duties, and Mother was grateful for this.

When the nights were cold Mother was forced to cover our beds with overcoats to help keep us warm because she didn't have enough blankets. The coats were heavy, but still they didn't keep us warm. Jean and Pat argued about who had more arm of a coat than the other did. I had my own bed, and John was in the cot next to Mother's bed in the other room. If the sirens sounded at night, which by now they invariably did, Mother rushed to get us up, put coats over our bed clothes and get us down to the shelter in the quickest possible time. I would be so sleepy when I was woken up that I would crawl back into bed as Mother was getting my siblings ready; which frustrated her. 'Tony! Come on, hurry up!' She was very jumpy at these times. Holding hands, Indian file, keeping close to the reservoir wall, we hurriedly moved towards the shelter. Often the moon shone an eerie light over the area and our breath left trails in the cold night air. Because I was so drowsy I would often forget to put on my boots. Walking over the stones outside left my feet hurting, which usually made me wide awake.

The shelter had a dank, fusty smell and the bedding was usually cold and damp to the touch. Mother lit the smelly paraffin heater, so we soon warmed up and fell asleep in our bunks, which were really comfortable. We always stayed there for the remainder of the night, even if the all-clear sounded. Mother said that it was too disruptive to take us back to the cottage. Many schoolchildren fell asleep at their desks after a night raid, and frequently the teachers would let them sleep on.

Six more raids took place in that June, causing fatalities, injuries and damage to buildings. The huge cast iron gates of our property were removed for the war effort and the space was blocked in. A wooden gate was installed instead, which was nearer to the cottage. Next to it was a concrete fresh water tank for emergency use only.

At the end of July the schools broke up for the summer holidays and my sister Jean was delighted to be home for six weeks. On the first Monday of the holiday Mother was in the wash house stoking the copper to get the water boiling for the sheets and whites. Father wore white collarless shirts, which he changed twice a week, but he wore a clean collar every day, attached with a front and back stud. We were as usual playing in front of the cottage when we heard the gate open. An army officer came striding up the path and so we all ran to Mother shouting. She came out of the wash house. The officer went up to her, stood to attention and saluted, 'Mrs Trevail?' Mother nodded affirmatively. 'I'm Lieutenant Colonel Northcott of the 16th Battalion Home Guard. Is your husband in please?'

'No, I'm afraid he's out on a job. Can I help you?'

'I'm afraid I have orders to commandeer your cottage for some of my Home Guard troops.'

Mother was dumbstruck for a moment before she blurted out, 'You can't. Where will we go? There are six of us including my husband.'

'Have you anyone that could take you in?'

'No, I can't think of anyone.'

'I'm terribly sorry but I have no alternative. It won't be for too long, I think. Perhaps you could talk it over with your husband when he comes home. I'll come again on Friday.'

When Father came home that afternoon Mother told him the news. He was livid but said, 'Well I suppose we don't have any choice. We'll have to live in the shelter until they go.'

Lieutenant Colonel Northcott returned on Friday and told them that his troops would be there the following Wednesday at 9 a.m. Mother, Father and we children commenced an exodus from the cottage with whatever was needed to make our stay as comfortable as possible. The troops duly moved in and slept on the floors, in our beds, on the stairs and in the cottage porch. They also slept in the wash house. For three weeks they carried out manoeuvres on the top of the reservoir, in the adjacent fields and all over Father's gardens, which were churned up like a quagmire from the soldiers crawling on their bellies, a few with rifles, but most of them making do with broomsticks and pieces of wood, held in front of them, advancing on an imaginary foe. Father was annoyed that his pride and joy, the gardens, were being ruined. Lieutenant Colonel Northcott assured him that all would be put back as before when the training was completed.

'I'll believe it when I see it,' said my irascible father.

However, we became very friendly with some of the soldiers and were given sweets from time to time. But we soon got tired of watching their games and carried on life as normal, playing our own games. Mother was permitted to collect water from the tap outside the wash house, whenever she needed it. It was very difficult for her to keep us washed, using a bucket and enamel bowl, and fed, using the paraffin heater as a cooker; but she managed well.

After three weeks the Home Guard left and true to their word they left the place as they had found it. They even tilled and planted the garden, which had been ruined, to the delight of Father.

In spite of the war we children managed to go out to play every day with our friends. If the siren sounded during the day, which wasn't very often at the start of the war, we were always within five minutes running distance of our shelters. My sister Jean had two friends, Pat Burridge and Sheila Bryant. My friends were Gerald Burridge, Peter Aze, Stewart Herring, Gordon Crimp and Bill Hammett, Gerald being my best friend. My younger sister's friends were Margaret Luscombe and Maureen Mellett, the latter being a beautiful dark haired girl whom I really liked. Most of my friends did as well. Maureen liked Gerald better than me. He had sandy hair and always wore a collar and tie. I was shorter and had black hair the same as she did. Gerald's father was a Dockyard policeman and rode a horse. That summer, the cattle had been taken away from Cundy's fields to the abattoir and so they were empty for us to play in. Although I was only four and a half, as long as Jean was around we were allowed in the fields. By going out into the lane at the rear of our cottage and through the five-barred wooden gate, we could get directly into the fields. There were two of them separated by a long hedge. They sloped towards the lane on one side and backed onto St. Aubyn's cemetery and a quarry on the other sides. In the first field there were two barns, one of which had a horse trough outside, which was a great attraction to my friends and me. The water in it was a little murky, but on a sunny day when the rays penetrated the water we could see strange wriggling worm-like creatures which seemed to swim about in a haphazard fashion. We made little boats to sail in it or threw stones in to splash each other.

The girls played gentler games like making mud pies or playing with their dolls and pretending to be little mothers. They also made daisy chains and put them on their heads to make themselves look like princesses.

My friends and I also prised up sun-baked cow pats for discus throwing competitions to see who could throw them the furthest. Jean shouted to me, 'I shall tell Father of you when he comes home.'

'Don't be a tell-tale tit,' I replied, knowing that Father might give me a clout across the head if I had been misbehaving.

After these competitions we washed our hands in the stagnant horse-trough water before going home. It never got rid of the smell of cow dung, which I quite liked. The girls thought that we were disgusting but we didn't care a hoot. Although there was an age difference we all got on well together. We built camps in the hedges and generally had a splendid time. If we got hungry we ran home to Mother and asked, 'Can we have something to eat please, we're starving?'

'Have you got hollow legs?' Mother would retort. 'What do you want? Fried snowballs or rabbit jam?'

'Something better please.'

She would cut a slice of bread and spread margarine over it, before scraping most of it off again to leave a thin layer. She then covered the margarine with white sugar and shook off the excess. 'There you are, a nice sugar sandwich. Now run away laughing.' I certainly did.

All my friends and I collected cigarette cards, known as 'fag' cards, which came in the packets of cigarettes. They depicted famous sportsmen, such as jockeys, cricketers and footballers, and all sorts of other subjects. We had a game where two boys would stand six cards up against a wall and each had a turn at 'flicking', which meant holding a card between the first two fingers and the thumb and shooting it at the cards which were stood up. If your card knocked any over, they would be yours. The game was over when all the cards had been collected up. Sometimes we stuck a piece of cardboard over the back of the fag card to make it stiffer which helped it to fly straighter. This was against the rules of the game and anyone caught had their cards confiscated.

Another favourite game we played was marbles, which we called 'alleys'. 'Brown Patch' was the best place for this because it was a piece of ground where the earth was hard and the undulations made it difficult to play. Mr Dean's house was near this patch and he was always coming out to tell us to play outside our own houses; but Brown Patch was the best place to play. I kept my alleys in an old sock, which had been darned a few times. The alleys had different names and some were prized more than others. I had agates, swirls, onion skins, blue tiger eyes, cat's eyes, Lutz, clears, opaques, Cornelions, big ones (which we called 'twicers' because you had to hit them twice to win them) and ball bearings, which we called 'ballbies'. We sometimes changed the alleys for shrapnel and played with these instead, but most of it went rusty very quickly, and because of its irregular shape, it never went where you wanted it to.

One hot day in August Jean and Pat, with her friends Maureen Mellett and Margaret Luscombe, were playing in the wash house. They were making mud pies and decorating them with daisies collected from Cundy's field. The bottom of the stable door was half-closed. Mother appeared with some home-made buns and lemonade on a tray. 'Jean, make sure that they all wash their hands first.'

I had been playing with my friends in front of the cottage and saw Mother give the girls something, so we went to the wash house to see what we were missing. 'Can we have some?'

'Where are your manners?' Jean said.

'Come on, don't be mean, give us some *please*,' we all shouted.

'All right, but you will have to wash your hands and sit in a circle.'

'Our hands are clean already,' Gerald said. We all looked at our brown-stained, grimy hands, which to us were perfectly acceptable.

'Don't wash, don't get,' said Jean in her most authoritative voice.

We turned on the outside tap and tried to wash off the grime, but with limited success. We then sat in a circle and were served off a doll's plate and cup and saucer. We had a wonderful tea party. But I couldn't keep my eyes off Maureen and blurted out, 'I want to marry you Maureen!'

'No it's Gerald's turn,' was the sharp reply.

I was hurt to the quick that she liked him better than me.

Jean gave Maureen an old piece of curtain for a veil and Pat scraped some daisies together with mud all over the stems and made a posy for her. Ted Rowe, another of my friends and a cousin of Maureen, conducted the marriage ceremony. Gerald had to kiss Maureen at the end of it and his face glowed bright red. The kiss was the final straw for me and, with a shout of rage, I trampled on all the mud pies and went into the lavatory and locked the door. I sat on the green seat, which had a split in it and pinched my bum, which really hurt. Father was always going to mend the seat but never got round to it. I could hear the girls whispering outside and knew that they were up to something. I felt fairly safe and looked at the squares of newspaper on the nail. (When I used the lavatory I derived a lot of pleasure looking for a picture of someone's face in the squares of newspaper so that I could wipe my bum on it.)

The whispering stopped and Jean pushed a hosepipe through the top of the door and shouted to someone, 'Turn it on.'

Water squirted through the hose and soaked me. I could not get out of the way because of the smallness of the space. I was irate and yelled, 'I will tell Father of you if you don't stop.' They were all laughing their heads off.

The water finally stopped and I emerged soaked to the skin. 'That will teach you, Tony,' they taunted. I looked at Maureen for sympathy but she was laughing as hard as the rest. Mother had come to see what was happening because of the noise and I was hauled indoors to be dried off.

The summer seemed to go on forever and it never rained, or so it seemed. There were twelve night raids in August and thirty-five people lost their lives. Father was kept very busy dealing with the fires and had seen some gruesome sights of carnage and death. Mother thought that these events made him drink more than normal. She was looking very gaunt and had dark rings around her eyes caused by worry and lack of sleep.

One Sunday lunchtime father came home late from the pub, having drunk too much, and was in a belligerent mood. 'I want my dinner,' he announced.

'Well it's all dried up,' Mother said as she put it in front of him.

He shouted, 'I'm not eating that!' and threw the plate to the floor where it broke, the contents spilling across the lino.

'Now look what you've done!' she cried.

'I want something to eat,' he bellowed.

'There's only bread and jam,' Mother replied.

'I give you good money for food. What do you do with it?'

'No, you don't give me good money. If you did, I wouldn't have had to do this.' She showed him her wedding finger, which just showed a white circle of flesh against her tanned skin, where her wedding and engagement rings had been.

'Where are your rings?' he uttered, his eyes glazing over.

Tears welled up in Mother's eyes. 'I had to pawn them, because I needed money for food; I did tell you but you wouldn't listen.'

'Well you shouldn't have,' Father said.

'I didn't have a choice. The children have got to eat and you won't go without anything.'

She was sobbing uncontrollably now. This seemed to bring Father to his senses and he staggered into the sitting room and sank heavily into his armchair, his hands cradling his head.

'What have I done?' He was silently weeping. 'It's this bleddy war that's done it. I'm sorry Vi. It won't happen again. I promise.'

Mother comforted him and then led him up the stairs to bed. On Monday morning, first thing, Father redeemed Mother's rings, which made her very happy. He turned over a new leaf and cut down on his drinking.

The summer holidays were by now coming to an end. In September I would be joining Jean at school. But I wasn't looking forward to it.

Chapter 10

On my first day at school Mother got me ready and, with Jean and me holding hands, John in the pram with Pat holding on to it and Mother pushing, we walked the 600 yards or so to the school gate. I was scared and didn't want to let go of Mother's hand. 'You'll be all right. And anyway Jean will see you at play time, won't you Jean?'

'Yes Mother.'

Miss Cree was my teacher. We all sat at little desks and she read our names out from a book. 'You answer "Present Miss Cree" when I call your name out.'

I didn't like her. She was an old spinster, short and fat, and she shouted at us. If someone did something wrong she ground her teeth and contorted her face into a vicious grimace as she scolded them. She ruled us with an iron rod and woe betide anyone who upset her.

In the first weeks we were provided with slates to write on, with little pieces of chalk. We wrote the alphabet and sung our two times tables. If the weather was dry we sometimes played in the sandpit, which was situated near the girl's toilet in the playground. The school day seemed to go on forever, especially as we had to sleep for a while in the afternoon, in little cots. I always looked forward to going-home time. I did not like school one little bit. Mother said that Christmas would soon be here and that was something to look forward to. I remembered last Christmas quite clearly, especially eating roast chicken, which I really loved.

At home Father enjoyed teasing me when we were having our meals and played cruel tricks. I very often fell asleep after eating and on many occasions he would shake me awake and say, 'Come on Tony, wake up! I've got some sugar for you. Open your mouth.'

I always fell for it and opened my mouth wide, very expectant. Father put the teaspoon in my mouth. 'Ugh!' He had put a pinch of salt on the spoon and I felt sick and spat it out. Father roared his head off.

'Don't be so cruel, John,' Mother said.

'What's wrong? It's only a bit of fun; it won't hurt him,' he retorted. 'I don't want him to grow up to be a sissy.'

Father pointed up at the flypaper pinned to the centre of the ceiling, covered in dead and dying flies. 'What's that up there Tony?' I always looked up; I never seemed to learn. Then he would place the teaspoon that he had been stirring his tea with on the back of my hand, which made me jump.

'John, for goodness sake leave the boy alone and don't be so cruel.'

'Oh don't be so soft Vi, I want him to be tough when he grows up.'

This was his sadistic streak coming out. The only way that I could get my own back on him was to touch his bald pate as I passed his chair and say 'Fly's skating ring!' and run out of the cottage. He was very sensitive about his hair loss and hated anyone making reference to it. 'I'll tan your backside when I catch you, you cheeky little bugger.'

On one occasion after tea when I did this, Father decided to chase me, which wasn't very often. I was in the lane by the time he reached the gate; but he lost his footing and came crashing down on one of the raised flower beds, gashing his arm, which began to spurt blood. I had nipped around the back of the cottage and climbed over the wall by the lavatory and made my way up the 'res', where I hid in the bushes so that I could see what was happening. The fall had knocked the wind out of him and he sat where he was. After a few minutes I watched him go back to the cottage holding his arm. I was scared stiff by now and was in a real quandary as to what to do. I decided that I would lower myself down into the bell shaped overflow pipe, because there I would be out of sight. But as I entered the pipe my knee became jammed and I couldn't move. I shouted at the top of my voice, 'Mother help! I'm stuck in the pipe.'

An hour went by. Then I heard Mother calling for me, 'Tony! Where are you? Everything will be all right.'

'Mother, I'm stuck in the pipe up the res!' This time she heard me and came running up the stony path to the top where she saw my head poking above the pipe.

'What are you doing in there, you stupid boy?'

'I was hiding from Father and now I'm stuck.'

By this time I was crying. My knee was hurting like mad. Mother leaned over the pipe and grabbed my arms, but it was no good. She started screaming for Father and he came on the scene quite soon. He was mad.

'Don't get on to him, just do something,' Mother said.

He rushed off and was soon back with a tin of axle grease. After liberally smearing my legs, he was able to release me. 'I'll speak to you later, my buck,' he said, glaring at me.

Father gave me a good tongue lashing the next morning at breakfast, which was much better than getting the back of his hand across my head, which always made me see stars. His arm was bandaged and there was a tinge of blood showing through. I dared not look at it. Father always used his hand to chastise us children.

We ate all our meals at the table in the dining room. An oil cloth covered the table; it had a bright green design. Jean, Pat and I sat on a bench against the wooden partition which separated the stairs from the room. Father sat at the head of the table; I sat next to him. Mother sat across from us with John in his high chair next to her. She had a long cane with a curved handle, which hung off the mantelpiece in the kitchen just behind where she sat, within easy reaching distance. If we were misbehaving at the table she only had to reach up and sweep it under the table to 'tickle our bare legs' as she called it; but it certainly stung, so we didn't call it a cane, we called it the 'tickler'. Jean and I used to break little pieces of the bottom of this tickler to make it shorter, hoping that eventually it wouldn't be able to reach our legs.

Mother said, 'I'm sure the tickler is getting shorter. Do you children know anything about it?'

'No Mother, honest we don't,' we all replied in unison.

We kept breaking pieces off until it was diminished to about six inches long and was useless. We were so naive that we never realised Mother knew all along what we were doing, but we thought that we were so clever.

Father had screwed little hooks under the mantelpiece to hang our gas masks, which were encased in cardboard boxes and string to carry them. He also hung his steel helmet on a hook too. We had to take the gas masks with us wherever we went. Jean, Pat and I had red rubber Mickey Mouse ones. The eyepieces were large and they had a long red rubber nose. We enjoyed wearing them and made rude noises by blowing hard into them which made the rubber vibrate against our cheeks. Mother told us off when we did this, but we did it all the more. Mother and Father had the 'civilian respirator', with elastic bands to keep it on the head. Baby John had a full body respirator into which he was placed and zipped up, his little legs protruding out of the bottom. There was a small pump on the side which Mother used to get air in. She could see him through a large Perspex window, but hated his having to be in it and was afraid that he would suffocate.

The gas masks had to be checked for leaks from time to time and, at school, a gas van would arrive. We had to line up, gas masks on and, six at a time, go into the back of the van. Just as we left the van we took our gas masks off and got a small whiff of mustard gas which made us gasp and our eyes water. It made us realise that we really had to look after our masks.

There had not been an air raid since 28 November. As Christmas was fast approaching we were rehearsing a Nativity play at school. All the classes were involved and I was to be a woodcutter in a sketch called 'The Little Fir Tree'.

Father made me a wooden axe and painted the handle brown and the head silver. I thought it was wonderful. Jean was chosen to play Mary, the Mother of Jesus.

Father was spending more time in his workshop where he had a treadle fret saw and all sorts of tools. I was told not to go down there and I wondered why, but was afraid to ask. Because my parents didn't have money to spare, Father was engaged in making all sorts of toys for us children and Mother too was busy at the Singer sewing machine working in the evenings after we had gone to bed. She was knitting a balaclava for me and various clothes for the girls. Unknown to us all, Father was making me a wooden sit-in train, the body of which was from a tree trunk. It had a T-shaped steering handle at the bottom of which were two chains that turned the front wheels (obtained from a pram). It was painted waterworks green. He had also made a wooden duck, which was pulled along behind it. Inserted into its wheels were pieces of orange inner tube which had been cut into the shape of webbed feet. When the duck was pulled along its feet made flapping sounds. These were all painted to look real.

Jean's present was a doll's house with a thatched roof made from shredded rope and glued on. Mother also made toys for Pat and John. All of these toys would be revealed on Christmas morning. Father was so clever with his hands that he made toys to order and were sold in Cooks, a small shop in Stoke village.

The play at school was progressing well and Jean knew her lines. My part was pretending to cut down some fir trees which were actually my friends dressed up. As I was cutting them down I had to shout, 'TIMBER!' Father coached me to do this properly. The play was held on the last day of term in the afternoon. I was scared at having to perform, but Mother said that I would be fine as Father had spent the time rehearsing it with me.

Mother came with Pat and John and felt very proud. Jean was word perfect; she was always dancing and singing; it seemed to come naturally to her. Everyone's parents were very supportive and clapped enthusiastically. Now it was our turn. The fir trees came on stage. As I stepped up I saw Mother with Pat and John, so I smiled and waved to them. Miss Cree hissed, 'Pay attention Tony!' I saw her at the side of the stage and her face was like thunder. I lost my nerve. I moved to the first tree and pretended to chop it down and in a barely audible voice said, 'Timber.'

Miss Cree hissed again, 'Louder! Louder!' I was so terrified that I quickly moved to the other two trees and did the same. The children began to giggle and Mother felt sorry for me. She was glad when it was all over.

When we were changing back stage Miss Cree grabbed me by the arm and brought her face close to mine so I could see the evil in her eyes. 'You spoilt the whole pantomime.' I started to cry and she let me go. 'I'll see you after Christmas,' she said through clenched teeth.

We broke up for the two-week Christmas holiday. Father always made a joke of breaking up for holidays and said that we would have to take a hammer and chisel to break up the school. I being very gullible, believed it to be true, knowing that if the school was broken up we would not have to go anymore.

The weather got much colder and rained almost every day. The cottage was always full of steam from the clothes that Mother put on the clothes horse in front of the fire. If it wasn't steam it was the smoke from Father's pipe which drifted from room to room in clouds. The sash windows in the cottage were very loose and rattled and Mother put cloths around them to help keep out the cold drafts. If it was particularly cold, Father shovelled some glowing embers from the sitting room fire and put them in our bedroom grate to try to take the chill off the room. It wasn't unusual to see our breath rising on winter mornings.

We were all happy to be away from school and started to prepare for Christmas. We made paper chains from crêpe paper and stuck them together with glue made from flour and boiling water. These chains were held up with drawing pins and hung from the picture rail to the centre of the room where the 60 watt bulb hung, emitting its yellow light. Mother put up a string of cardboard imitation Chinese lanterns which spelled 'A Merry Christmas'. Jean and I had been collecting holly from the hedge near the cemetery and we also found some mistletoe.

We hung these around the room and they looked very cheerful. Father had managed to get a small Christmas tree and placed the root in a fire bucket with earth to keep it in place. The bucket was covered in crêpe paper and the tree was decorated with cheap trinkets which, to us children, were marvellous.

Father had a few days off and on Christmas Eve in the morning he said to me, 'I want you to help me in the shed to get the chicken ready.'

Mother said, 'He's a bit young for that, isn't he?'

'He'll be all right.'

'What have I got to do Father?'

'You'll see in a minute, come on.'

We went to the workshop and Father showed me which chicken was to be killed for tomorrow's dinner. I felt very scared. He had a meat hook hanging on some binder twine from one of the rafters and underneath he put one of the red fire buckets, which he had emptied. He went out to the chicken coop and came back with the biggest chicken that we had. It was squawking and flapping its wings. He tied some more binder twine around its feet and hung it on the meat hook. I was horrified and wanted to leave. 'Stay there and watch, you'll have to do this when you're a bit older.'

He took his leather cutting knife and holding on to the chicken's head, forcing its beak open, he cut the roof of its mouth. Blood poured out into the bucket. The chicken flapped furiously and he let go of it. The blood spurted in an arc and went across my face. I cried out as some of it went into my mouth. It felt very warm and I spat it out. Father told me to pass him a wooden mallet, which was nearby. He then hit the chicken across the head, which finished it off. The flow of blood gradually eased off to a drip. He passed me a piece of rag to wipe the blood off.

'Right, now stop being a baby and pass me that small bath over there. I'll show you how to pluck it.' I was feeling sick and rushed outside, bringing up my porridge on the garden. 'Pass me the bath,' he shouted.

I wanted to run to Mother but Father insisted that I watch him. He deftly plucked the feathers off whilst the bird was still warm. 'Come here and you try it.'

I tentatively plucked out some feathers at the same time looking at the chicken's head which was lolling about, its eyes still open, looking back at me accusingly.

'There, that wasn't too bad was it?'

After the plucking he cut off its head and with his pincers cut the feet off. He took one of the severed feet in his hand and, pulling the white tendons, made the claws go in and out. (I soon got over the experience and as the years passed by would wring the chicken's necks but would not slit their beaks.)

'Here, you can have this one,' he said, as he gave me a foot.

I immediately ran up to the cottage and, seeing Pat, chased her with the chicken's foot. Mother was delighted with the chicken and said that it would make quite a few meals. She started to clean it, pulling out the giblets which she said would make lovely gravy, and then stuffed it with sage and onion. She sewed up the hole and said that Father would have the Parson's Nose, pointing to the bottom. Jean and I said, 'Ugh!' together.

Mother had been baking for weeks before Christmas and had made a cake and a pudding with silver threepenny bits in the mixture. On Christmas Eve she made all sorts of goodies so that the festival would be a joyous occasion. We were all excited because we were told that Father Christmas would be visiting us in the night if we had been good children and that he would be bringing presents. Mother got us ready for bed in front of a roaring fire which Father had started with the paraffin from his blowlamp. He told us that the paraffin was magic water, which of course we all believed. Then he started getting ready to go to the pub. He tucked a towel in his collarless shirt and started to shave, at the same time whistling happily.

'Please don't be late back tonight, John. I want us to do it together,' Mother said with an imploring look.

'I told you I will be back by ten o'clock, and that's the time it will be.'

Baby John had been put in his cot earlier and was fast asleep. Mother gave Jean, Pat and me clean pillowslips to put over our shoulders as we went up the stairs to bed. The blackout had been put over all the windows and the house was very dark when the lights were off. I hated the dark and often, when in bed, I strained my eyes and could make out things moving which made me very frightened. We put our pillowslips at the bottom of our beds and Mother tucked us up.

'Now remember, if you're awake, Father Christmas won't come.'

'We won't be Mother, but what if there's an air raid?' Jean asked.

'We go to the shelter as quickly as possible.' She kissed us and bade us goodnight.

At two o'clock in the morning I woke up to the sound of rustling. Mother said, 'Go back to sleep, he hasn't been yet.' I settled back down, but about an hour later I awoke and crept to the bottom of my bed and felt my pillow slip. It was full of objects, which I felt to try to work out what they were. I could smell oranges in the bottom of the slip. Jean was awake now and she did the same.

'Father Christmas has been and we've got lots of things,' she whispered. We dragged the slips up in our beds to await the light.

At five o'clock it was still dark and we got out of bed and put the light on. Pat was now awake and we all looked at each other's presents. My train was at the foot of the bed, which I had missed in the night. We were really pleased with all the presents we had. They were all homemade. Mother had made me an aeroplane. Jean had her doll's house, and Pat had woollen dolls and a wooden painted bracelet with elastic threaded through it. There were other small trinkets. We were very pleased and decided to go into Mother and Father's room to share the good news. Baby John was sitting up in his cot awake but they were asleep but soon awoke. They were surprised that we had so many things and for the next hour we shared our treasures with them.

Father decided to get up and make the fire in the sitting room. We had a wonderful Christmas Day playing with our toys and Mother put the chicken in the oven quite early. At 12.30 we sat down to our Christmas dinner. Auntie Ivy joined us for the rest of the day. She showed Mother and Father the last letter that Jack had sent and intimated that he was going abroad soon. She was sad, but, being with our family, she enjoyed herself.

The chicken was delicious and Father put some brandy over the home-made Christmas pudding and lit it. We cheered. Later we played card games and listened to the King's speech on the wireless. We had tea and played housy-housy (bingo); Father was the caller. The numbers were put into a cloth bag and we had paper tickets with our fifteen numbers on. He passed the bag to one of us and said, 'Give 'em a good shake.' Then the game began.

'All the eights, two fat ladies. Two little ducks, twenty-two. Kelly's eye, number one. All the sixes, clickety click. Four O, blind 40.' This went on until someone crossed a line off or had a full house. This was such good fun and we played for sweets, which Mother had made. We went to bed thoroughly exhausted but very contented.

Over the rest of the holiday, we were able to play with our toys outside if the weather was clement. It was the best Christmas in the whole world. But soon we had to return to school; and the air raids returned in earnest. Thankfully Miss Cree seemed to have forgotten my faux pas in the play.

Chapter 11

Jack Lambert had been on the troopship for three weeks. There were thousands of men crammed on the ship, like sardines in a tin, and tempers were getting frayed. He had been transferred to the 1st Gloucester Regiment under the leadership of Lieutenant Colonel C. E. K. Bagot who had only commanded the regiment for a few short months, but was proving to be an excellent leader. Two months previous to embarkation, Jack had been engaged in jungle warfare training but, although he enjoyed it, did not relish the thought of going overseas. The troops were very bored, with not much to do on the ship, except listen to lectures interspersed with a walk around the deck twice a day. The weather was getting better as they were nearing their destination and the warm sunshine was a welcome relief from the drab weather of England.

Jack had teamed up with another private named Peter Holmes whose nickname was Sherlock, after the famous detective. Only a few months before both men had received cholera and yellow fever injections and were told that they would be shipping out to somewhere hot, which they now knew was Burma. Because of the close proximity of the men with one another there were a few altercations, and Jack had been involved in a few, though they were usually just a shouting match or a shove here or there.

One morning Jack and Sherlock collected their water for shaving. Jack was about to lather up when a tall muscular soldier pushed past him and knocked his water on the deck. He just continued without saying a word. Jack was incensed and made after him. 'Oi! You just knocked my shaving water over.'

‘Well, go and get some more,’ was the reply.

‘No, you give me yours.’

‘Get lost.’ He pushed Jack in the chest.

Jack saw a red mist rise up before his eyes and instinctively hit the soldier in the solar plexus. The man crumpled to the deck, the air rushing out of his lungs like a punctured tyre. Jack walked away with the man’s water and poured it into his Billy Can and started to shave. He could see the man out of the corner of his eye as the man’s mates lifted him to his feet. As he was catching his breath he looked at Jack with hatred in his heart. He wasn’t finished with Jack and looked around for a suitable weapon. His eyes fixed on an open cut-throat razor nearby. He grabbed it and made a lunge at Jack. Although Jack saw him coming he was too slow to dodge out of the way and received a slash to the back of his head. He didn’t feel any pain, but felt something warm running down his neck and back. The men gasped. Jack grabbed the man’s wrist that was holding the razor with his left hand and punched him in the jaw, knocking him out cold. His mates threw some cold water over him to bring him round.

Sherlock said, ‘You will have to get that stitched Jack.’

‘Help me to the sick bay please Sherlock.’

Jack had lost quite a bit of blood and was feeling a little faint. Sherlock took him to the sick bay. Jack told the medical officer that he had slipped and hit his head. He received twelve stitches. The other man recovered and things settled down once more.

On 7 September 1941 the ship put in at the harbour of Rangoon, where the men disembarked. Jack and Sherlock were ferried with the rest of the Gloucesters to a training camp about thirty miles from the Battalion Headquarters at Mingaladen. They were under the command of Captain Johnson and soon the men began more rigorous training in the jungle and in the difficult terrain about their camp. They had all been issued with light-weight khaki uniforms and topi helmets, and they sweated profusely in the hot and sticky atmosphere. They were taught survival techniques, should they get lost in the jungle, as well as how to deal with snakebites and which plants they could eat and which were poisonous. On 1 December Jack and Sherlock joined 'B' company and were billeted at the headquarters. It was just a few days later that Japan entered the war by bombing the American Fleet at Pearl Harbor.

Jack and Sherlock were put on patrol duties at the airport in Mingaladen, which was soon attacked by Japanese Aichi dive-bombers. Bombs rained down and Jack's rifle was no match for them. Rangoon took a battering too. Two days later as 'A' company was repairing bomb craters, they were caught out in the open as the Japanese attacked again. One man was killed and several suffered injuries. The battalion was not well equipped but due to the brilliant initiation of its officers and men, acquired much equipment and vehicles which had been abandoned after heavy bombing raids, earlier. The men had two Italian Breda machine guns with mortars and shells. Jack had got himself a Bren Gun and clips of shells and, as no one seemed to mind, he hung on to them. He still had his Lee–Enfield .303 rifle.

On the 17th the battalion was mobilised and the civilians who were attached to the Gloucesters were sent to Maymyo, further north. Christmas was just a few days off and the men had been promised a traditional Christmas dinner. The troops just couldn't imagine where the cooks would get such fare as there was a war on and food was very scarce as they had already experienced. They thought they would end up with bully beef and hard tack biscuits. However, they need not have worried because, under the guidance and supervision of Company Quartermaster Sergeant Ballenger, the cooks were at their ranges preparing turkeys, Christmas puddings and all the trimmings. The dinner was a huge success and Bagot commended Ballenger for his efforts. Jack and Sherlock stuffed themselves. They were served by NCOs and officers, as was the custom.

* * *

Rangoon had been severely damaged by the air raids and the Gloucesters had the unenviable task of burying the dead who were left to rot in the streets. The 15th Japanese Army led by general Iida had made inroads into Burma. General Sir Harold Alexander, the British Commander in Chief, ordered the evacuation of Rangoon. He had decided that because of the strength of the Japanese he would proceed to Prome and the Burma oil fields. The 1st Gloucesters were chosen to protect the rear of the long column as the men were fit and had a good knowledge of jungle warfare.

The column moved off and on the first day marched to Taukkyan, where they were halted by a Japanese roadblock. Bagot took 'B' company to sort it out. Jack had his rifle, the Bren gun and some hand grenades; Sherlock just had his rifle and some hand grenades. Bagot called a meeting with the company.

'This is our initial plan of action. Number 10 Platoon will advance towards the enemy up the left-hand side of the road. Number 12 Platoon will go up on the right-hand side and two Bren Carriers from 'C' company will try to flush them out. Any questions? Right off we go and best of luck.'

Jack felt as if his heart would explode and Sherlock looked terrified as they cautiously advanced in single file on the right-hand side. The roadblock consisted of some barrels and some large tree branches. Suddenly, they came under a severe hail of machine-gun fire; one man dived to the side of the road. Many were hit and lay on the ground moaning.

'Are you all right Sherlock?' Jack hissed.

'Yes mate,' was the curt reply.

They started to return fire. It was pandemonium: gunfire, men screaming in agony and the screech of birds and animals from the jungle.

Meanwhile Number 10 Platoon, which was slowly advancing, came under heavy fire. The two Bren Carriers were speeding down the road and, as the first one approached the roadblock, it was hit by a mortar shell which killed all the crew. A Japanese anti-tank gun fired at the other Bren Carrier, but this one returned fire and many Japanese soldiers were killed. But then that carrier too received a direct hit, killing most of the crew and wounding others. But Phylatoff, the White Russian driver, wasn't hurt and like a maniac raced to the first Bren Carrier and picked up the survivors and took them to safety with the allies.

Jack and Sherlock were pinned to the road still, but were returning fire. Lieutenant Williams commanding their platoon was the only officer not wounded. There had been about fifteen Japanese manning the anti-tank gun, but that number had now been reduced. Bagot took nine men from 'B' company and advanced again. Some renegade Burmese opened up, killing two of Bagot's men, leaving him with only seven. They immediately returned fire, killing some more. Bagot lost another four men soon after and all three lobbed hand grenades at the men manning the anti-tank gun, killing some and sending the rest scurrying for cover. Bagot left these three men covering the anti-tank gun, in case the enemy tried to man it again. He retraced his steps down the road to collect the rest of 12 Platoon, but the Japanese made a counter-attack and forced him and his men to retreat.

Jack and Sherlock knew that they had killed at least one Japanese soldier and the adrenaline rush that they were experiencing was euphoric. The situation was a place of terror; the cacophony of battle noise was horrendous, with men screaming in agony and the sound of explosions and gunfire; and there was the smell of cordite and the dense steaming jungle. Jack was terrified to start with but, in the middle of the action, with adrenalin pumping, he lost his fear, as most of the men did on both sides. Bagot assessed that there were about 500 Japanese troops that were stopping them and another battalion behind that one. His men dug in and the Italian Breda guns and mortars concentrated fire once again on the roadblock, and Jack and Sherlock raked the trees for snipers. Just then the jungle caught fire in the vicinity of the roadblock and, in the ensuing confusion, the 4/12 Frontier Force which had been put under Bagot's command advanced up the road. But they didn't make much impression on the enemy.

Night came and during this time reinforcements arrived. 'A' company came up from Syriam, 'C' company came from Rangoon and one remaining platoon of 'B' company came up from army headquarters. Two other units from the 17th Indian Division and the 7th Hussars also came. The battalion was up to full strength and now stood a much better chance against the enemy. Early on the tanks were brought up to attack the roadblock and, with covering fire from the flanks, some headway was made.

Jack, Sherlock and three other soldiers under the command of Lieutenant Hollington were patrolling carefully through the jungle when they came upon a Japanese machine-gun nest. They froze in their tracks, afraid that they had been spotted. They were lucky: they hadn't been. They carefully sunk to their bellies onto the floor of the jungle. Hollington whispered, 'Listen carefully. Lambert and you Holmes get into position behind that tree trunk on the right flank and you three advance on the left flank. I'll give you covering fire, if you need it. Just watch for my signal and don't fire until you see it. All understood?' They all nodded. 'Best of luck.'

Jack felt that he needed all the luck in the world. The adrenaline was once more pumping as he and Sherlock crawled on their stomachs and got into position behind the tree trunk. Jack had the Bren Gun slung over his back and his rifle in his hands. They were in a dip in the ground, which allowed them to see the enemy without being seen. Jack slowly manoeuvred the Bren Gun into position and lined up the sight on the unsuspecting Japanese. Sherlock whispered, 'Wait for Hollington's signal, Jack!'

They could see that the other men were in position. Hollington gave the signal and all hell broke out. Jack's Bren Gun rattled and a soldier disappeared from view. The enemy soon returned fire. Jack's gun stopped working due to a gas lock, so he quickly changed to his rifle. The Japanese saw their position and bark started to fly off the tree trunk. 'Get your head down Sherlock.' Sherlock's head was already pressed into the dirt. Hollington and the other men killed the rest of the Japanese soldiers. Jack shook Sherlock and said, 'It's all right. You can get up now, it's all over.' Sherlock had a very frightened look on his face.

They all moved cautiously towards the machine-gun nest and for the first time saw the enemy at close quarters, albeit dead. The sight was terrible. One soldier's face was missing; another's entrails were hanging out. It was an awful experience. One of Hollington's men vomited into the bushes. Another man said, 'Ain't war bloody 'orrible. I don't know how much more of this I can stand.'

Sherlock said, 'You'll be all right mate; but we didn't start it did we?'

Lieutenant Hollington said, 'Well done men. Let's rejoin the others.'

The cost of this first serious action was totted up. Three officers had been killed and three wounded; seventeen other ranks had been killed and 23 wounded. 'C' company had been reduced to fewer than twenty men, so it had to be brought up to strength by transferring fifty men from other companies.

The column headed north again, the Gloucesters guarding the rear. This continued for a week without further engagement with the enemy. It was hot and very humid and everyone was footsore and weary. On 16 March Bagot received news that a battalion of Japanese was going to camp in the village of Letpaden the very next day. He decided to ambush them; however some Burmese collaborators heard about this and told the Japanese not to enter the village. So Bagot tried another ploy to convince the enemy that they were leaving the area. He sent a detachment of the Burma Frontier Force into the village with their lorries and equipment, where they unloaded everything. Some hours later they made a big show of packing up and moving out again. Bagot hoped that the collaborators would be taken in and inform the enemy. It had the desired effect and on the morning of the 19th, at four in the morning, the Japanese came back into the village. Bagot was informed and put his plan into action. A small platoon under the leadership of Lieutenant Sibly would approach the village to engage the enemy. Whilst this was going on, the main attack would come from the rear, to surprise the enemy. Sibly approached with his vehicles, leaving them with the drivers and approaching on foot with Sergeant Biggs and the rest of the platoon. As they went a little further along the roads they met an enemy patrol and engaged them in some vicious action, which sent them on the run. At that moment Sibly heard gunfire from the location of his lorries outside the village. He left Biggs in charge of the platoon and went back to help the drivers. The enemy was soon dispersed. Soon after, Biggs and the small platoon were completely surrounded and Sibly was unable to assist them.

Meanwhile 'D' Company had assembled at the rear of the village with eight mortars mounted on armoured cars and four machine guns. Two captains, 'Crusty' Christensen and 'Lakri' Wood gave the command to open fire. Mortar shells rained down on the village and an almost solid wall of lead caused the enemy to run for cover into the relative safety of the dense jungle. Some of the enemy were defending the village schoolhouse, but Dick Johnson of Company HQ lobbed a hand grenade through the window which made the enemy rush out of every opening in the building to escape, only to be met by the cold steel of the allies' bayonets, killing them all. Jack, Sherlock and the rest of their platoon were making their way up the main village road. They met the enemy and were engaged in hand to hand fighting, many of whom they killed. Jack's thoughts returned briefly to bayonet practice: this was the real thing and it was terrifying.

Now the enemy was on the run and 'D' Company chased the remaining men into the jungle. Jack had killed two more with his Bren and felt invincible. Sergeant Biggs, though, had not fared so well after Sibly had left. They had made a gallant stand but were outnumbered and decided to make a run for it, taking their wounded with them. They made it to a river valley and sought refuge in a ruined house. There they were confronted by another Japanese patrol. In the ensuing battle they ran out of ammunition and were captured. They were transported to a POW camp and spent the rest of the war in terrible conditions of suffering and deprivation.

The allies regrouped and marched for eight days just past Paungde in order to get some well-earned sleep. But no sooner had they fallen asleep, or so it seemed, than Bagot received a communication that the Japanese were entering Paungde from the west. The men were awakened at once and, after eating a hasty meal, got ready to make a surprise attack on the enemy. Jack was so tired that he felt he could have slept for a week.

At eight o'clock the whole battalion attacked. 'A' and 'D' left their transport, and under the covering fire of mortars went on foot. Jack had somehow got separated from his platoon and joined 'A' Company. The Japanese were hiding everywhere in the town. Jack had his rifle slung across his back and his Bren Gun at the ready. His marksmanship, which had been noted early on in his army career, was to be his salvation. He managed to shoot a sniper in a tree and return fire into a bamboo hut, into which someone threw a Molotov cocktail which set it on fire. Soon after an enemy soldier came rushing outside screaming. His uniform was on fire from head to toe and he blindly ran in Jack's direction. Jack loosed off a round, which killed him instantly. Jack's nostrils inhaled the stench of burning human flesh and his stomach heaved. Bullets were dancing around him, which brought him to his senses. He continued the fight.

'A' Company was now pinned down by enemy fire from a house. Jack was a little behind the main body of men, and out of the corner of his eye he saw three of the enemy setting up a firing position. Without any thought for his own safety, he stood up and screaming at the top of his voice charged towards them firing his Bren Gun as he ran, killing them all.

The enemy resistance was fierce and Bagot was forced to withdraw to a railway crossing near Padigong, a few miles away, where they reformed. They were to get some tank support but in the night they were attacked again. 'D' company was surrounded and under the command of Captain Johnson, who fought a long and bloody battle. Jack went with the rest of the battalion to a position north of Prone. The Gloucesters took the role of leading the rear guard of the brigade. The Japanese attacked again and they were caught between the main column and the rear of the column. They were held up by roadblocks and were being dive bombed by the enemy. Captain Johnson had rejoined the allies after extricating himself and his men from their previous action.

Jack was advancing through less dense jungle, still bringing up the rear, when he saw a movement in the trees about twenty yards ahead. He brought up his rifle to take aim.

When he woke up he didn't know where he was. He saw a woman in white, a nurse. 'Where am I?'

The nurse came over. 'You've been wounded, not seriously. You're in the field hospital.'

Jack felt some pain in his head and realised that he must have been shot. The sniper's bullet had run a furrow across his scalp, which needed thirty-four stitches. He felt nauseous. He heard that Bagot had also been wounded and was in hospital, against his wishes. His friend Sherlock had taken a bullet in the chest, which was lodged in his spine. Unbeknown to Jack he was awaiting surgery in another ward.

After a couple of days Jack was well enough to leave his sick bed. He was able to give some comfort to other soldiers who were badly injured. He made enquiries about his friend and was told that he had been injured and was in the hospital. He went to visit Sherlock who was recovering in a ward after an operation to remove the bullet from his spine. However, the surgeon could not remove it because of its position. Jack didn't easily recognise Sherlock at first. He just saw another pale-faced soldier in a bed. Sherlock was lucid but in great pain.

'How are you mate?' Jack whispered.

'I'll manage Jack.'

He had been given morphine for the pain but it was wearing off. A little dribble of blood was at his lips. Blood was seeping through the bandages around his chest. Jack could see that he was in a bad way and a lump formed in his throat. A nurse came and administered some more morphine. Sherlock dozed off.

'How bad is it?' he asked the nurse.

'I'm afraid it's very bad. He's had his lung removed and he's paralysed from the waist down.'

'Will he make it?'

'Probably, but he'll never walk again.'

Jack was devastated.

Sherlock was to be sent back to Blighty. Jack went to see him and said that he would soon be back out to fight another day.

'Thanks mate, but you know that'll never be. You see they've told me that I'll never walk again and I can't face that.' His eyes filled with tears. 'I couldn't bear being in a wheelchair for the rest of my life.'

'But you'll be going home to green fields, cold rain and decent grub!'

Sherlock fell asleep and Jack said, 'I'll see you tomorrow.'

But Jack never saw his friend again. On the troopship taking him home he put the muzzle of his rifle in his mouth and blew his brains out.

* * *

On 13 April the 1st Gloucesters, reduced to two companies, made it to Yenangyaung where some heavy fighting took place. Jack's flesh wound was healing well and he was back in the thick of it. The enemy had them outnumbered again. The two companies were split into small commando-type units and Jack was in one of these. Their task was to destroy some oil tanks at Yenangyaung, which was done successfully, with some of the groups meeting enemy aggression.

Bagot had rejoined the battalion, after being patched up, and rounded up all the groups. On the 27th at Shwebohe he formed the men into two rifle companies. They advanced towards Mandalay. They were poorly equipped, having had to give up some mortars and other weapons to other units. Jack still had his Bren and Lee–Enfield .303. When an officer earlier was going round the company looking for weapons he had had to hide his Bren, saying that it had been lost some time earlier. The Gloucesters were down to three Bren Guns – of which Jack's was one – nine Thompson sub-machine guns and a few lorries. The rest was made up of rifles and one anti-tank rifle. Bagot's men left Mandalay and were heading towards Kalewa. The enemy was advancing towards Kalewa too and had to be stopped because if they reached the River Chindwin before the allies, there was a good chance that their escape route would be cut off. Jack was sent with Captain Niblet and two companies of the 1st Gloucesters to Monwa to cut off the advancing Japanese. There was already a battle going on when they arrived, with the Burma Rifles engaging the enemy. Jack was following up the rear of the company and become separated from the rest of the men. As he made his way stealthily through the jungle, he was heading towards the top of a ridge. As he reached the top, a Japanese soldier confronted him. Before Jack had time to fire his rifle, the soldier stuck him in the chest with his bayonet. Jack, losing consciousness, rolled back down the ridge and into dense undergrowth, blood pouring from his wound. The enemy soldier made off into the jungle, sure that he had killed the Englishman.

Chapter 12

The blitz intensified and on many nights there was more than one air raid; we were spending more and more time in the shelter. There was usually a hubbub going on in the wardens' post next door; the telephone rang incessantly and we heard the muffled voices of the wardens as they received and gave information. A Bofors gun had been positioned in the back lane opposite the two shelters and when that was firing it was deafening. We hardly slept at all and were always tired out. Above the cacophony of these noises was the strange droning sound of the German bombers, which even to the stout hearted wrought fear in their souls. Mother was particularly affected by all of this and would shake.

The gas and electricity supplies were severed on more than a few occasions and we all had to make do until they were restored. The City Hospital had been damaged a couple of times and the patients were evacuated to other hospitals in Devon and Cornwall. Because of the fire devastation caused by incendiary bombs, the Auxiliary Fire Service tenders were repeatedly taking water from the reservoir pipes in the back lane, whilst Father supervised. The death toll was rising, as were the injuries to the populace of Plymouth.

One night in February Mother was awakened by the 'crump crump' of bombs exploding and quickly got us children out of bed. 'Quickly, get dressed. We have to go down to the shelter, there's a raid on. I just heard some bombs going off.'

'I'm too tired Mother; I want to stay in bed,' I cried, rubbing my eyes.

'Tony, get up at once! Do you want the Germans to drop a bomb on you?'

So I jumped out of bed and Mother led us out of the cottage towards the shelter. We knew what to do because we had done it so many times before.

The raiders approaching siren had not been sounded for some reason and we heard later that many people lost their lives because of this error. Father was on fire watch duty that night in the Ford district and got caught in the thick of it. A bomb exploded nearby and he was blown twelve feet into a doorway nearby, where he lost consciousness for a few minutes. When he regained his senses, he was choking in a dust storm caused by the collapse of the buildings around him. He felt himself to see if he was injured. His helmet was dented and he sustained a few scratches, but wasn't badly injured.

The bombers passed by and there followed an eerie quietness all around. As the dust clouds settled, he cautiously made his way down the street towards the devastation. Just in front of him was a man in pyjamas staggering around in a dazed state. A dog was whining nearby.

'Are you all right mate?' Father enquired.

'That was my house there,' the man said, pointing to a pile of smouldering rubble.

He was wearing an overcoat over his striped pyjamas. Father wondered how anyone could have survived that without sustaining a scratch. Father helped him away from the destruction. He was the only person that could be seen. Father asked him, 'Were you in the house?'

'No, I was in the Anderson shelter in the back garden.'

'Where's the rest of your family?'

'I haven't got any family. I live on my own.'

'You've had a very fortunate escape. Come to think of it, so have I. But I just wonder how many are under that lot,' he said, pointing back to the flattened houses. Father started to move some rubble in the hope that someone might be rescued.

'I'll help you,' the man said; but Father sat him down and told him that the emergency services would soon be there and would look after him.

The bells of the appliances could be heard in the distance getting louder as they approached the area of destruction. Then Father saw an arm poking out of the rubble and immediately started to remove bricks and slates with his bare hands. He pulled out the body of a young girl and laid her gently on the rubble. She looked so peaceful. He said later that she didn't have a mark on her. The appliances arrived and Father was told to go home and that they would deal with everything.

People had been buried under tons of debris and over the course of the next few days their bodies were dug out. There were eleven in total. Father was greatly affected by the horrible scenes he witnessed on that occasion. He returned to our shelter, covered in dust, in the early morning. We were all tucked up in our bunk beds, but were all awake because more German bombers were passing overhead. Just after he arrived we heard a deafening explosion. One of the wardens next door shouted, 'That sounded like a parachute mine.'

'That wasn't too far away,' another said.

Father whispered to Mother, 'Vi, I've seen some awful sights tonight.'

Mother quickly interjected, putting her hands over her ears, 'Don't tell me, I don't want to hear it.'

'I'm sorry Vi, I just didn't think,' he said, brushing himself down as best as he could.

'It's bad enough, without you telling me horrible things. Can't you go outside to brush yourself down? You're filling the shelter with dust.'

We children managed to get some sleep before the all-clear siren sounded; but Mother and Father were the only ones to hear it.

At six o'clock the next morning we returned to the cottage. Father went into the sitting room and slumped down in his armchair, falling asleep immediately. Mother covered him with a coat. She then made us our porridge and took us upstairs to get us ready for school. She had to push hard to get our bedroom door open. Then she screamed out, which woke Father.

'What is it?' he shouted, as he came rushing in.

We all looked in disbelief. The room was covered in masonry and dust covered everything. There was an enormous hole in the back wall, and there, lying on our bed, which had collapsed under the weight, was a huge piece of granite in the shape of a cross. It was obvious that it was the headstone of a grave.

'What if the children had been in bed? They'd have been injured, or even killed,' Mother bawled.

She looked heavenward and said a silent prayer. 'What a mess. The children can't sleep in here tonight.'

'It's back to the shelter again, until this lot is repaired,' said Father. 'It's a good job you woke up, especially as the ruddy siren didn't sound last night.'

Jean and I were excited by all of this and couldn't wait to get to school to tell anyone who would listen. Father carried the cross outside and put it on the concrete water tank for all to see. Mother took days to clear up the rubble and dust. We found out later that the parachute mine had exploded in St. Aubyn's cemetery, only 500 yards away.

The hole in the wall had caused long fracture cracks to appear around it, which looked like the body and legs of a huge spider. The corporation repaired the hole and filled the cracks with pitch to stop the rain coming in; but it made the cottage look ugly. We had to sleep in the shelter until the room was made habitable.

There was an uproar from the people of Plymouth as to why the siren had not been sounded. But officials gave more of an excuse than an answer.

By now the raids were increasing in intensity and on many nights a lorry took us and others from Stoke to a little village called Milton Coombe where we bedded down in the village hall. The lorry trundled at a snail's pace across the countryside and we were fascinated by the blackness of the night and the myriad of stars we observed. It was so quiet there, but not enough to drown out the drone of the enemy bombers and the exploding bombs raining down more death and destruction on Plymouth.

Now and again Auntie Ivy came with us, if she was visiting. She shared the letters she received from Uncle Jack with us, although she had not heard from him in a long time. She had a couple of photographs showing him in his khaki uniform with a bush hat on his head. He looked very smart. I really liked Uncle Jack; he was my hero.

After a night in the village hall, we would be given hot cocoa and a margarine sandwich and sent on our way. One warm morning as we were waiting for the lorry to take us back, I saw a snake on a dry stone wall curled up in the sun. I had never seen a snake before and froze, shouting for Mother. A man came over and said, 'Don't move son and you'll be all right. I won't be a minute.' He came back with a stick and managed to lift it to a safe distance, where he deposited it in the hedge. 'You were lucky there son, that was an adder. If it had bitten you, you would have gotten very ill.' I was still rooted to the spot.

This was the final straw for Mother and she asked Father if we could go somewhere to get away from the air raids and bombings. She seemed to be always crying. Father explained, 'If you were to be evacuated somewhere you know that I couldn't go with you.'

'I know that, but it's the children I'm worried about.' She broke down crying again.

'All right Vi, I'll see what I can do. Now calm down and stop crying. What will the children think?'

Mother looked at us and cried all the more. We tried to comfort her by putting our arms around her, but she just could not get the mental picture out of her head of us children lying on the bed with that granite cross on top of us, covered in blood, dead.

Father's niece, Olive, married to Bill Jones who was in the Police Reserve, heard that there was to be an evacuation of mothers and their children to Torquay, a seaside town on the 'English Riviera'. The Jones had three children: Stanley, the eldest, who was eight years old; Madeline, nicknamed Maddy, who was six; and Evelyn, nicknamed Ebby, who was three. Bill ran a vegetable business and made deliveries with his horse and cart. Fortunately he had arranged for Mother and us children to be on the evacuation list. Mother was feeling elated at the thought of leaving the blitz. (In March, Plymouth suffered some of the worst air raids of the war so far.)

On the day that we were to be evacuated, Monday 24 March 1941, Mr Keast, a friend of the family, arranged to take us and our meagre luggage to St. Mathias Church on North Hill, where an old charabanc was waiting to take us and other families to Torquay. Mother had been told to bring only essentials for our family, so she filled a couple of battered suitcases with as much as she could force in. Jean and I had sat on the lids so that Mother could latch them. Somehow Olive Jones had managed to take her portable sewing machine with her. The husbands had been allowed to accompany their families, which was a great help. Olive, a member of the Salvation Army, was the same age as Mother and they got on very well with each other.

As we left Plymouth we were very excited, as it was the first time that we had been in a charabanc and treated it as a new adventure. Father sat with Bill Jones and asked him, 'What is the name of this place we're going?'

Bill took out a scrap of paper and read, 'Eagles Cairn, Grafton Road, off Braddons Hill.'

'Don't much like the sound of it, but we'll see. Best wait until we see it before we condemn it.'

The charabanc rumbled and rattled along with clouds of smoke billowing from its exhaust pipe. Mother wasn't a good traveller: the smell of the exhaust as well as the oil and the winding roads made her feel very ill and at one point, along the winding roads of Devon, the driver had to stop to let her alight so she could be sick in the hedgerow. Jean helped her back on. Her face had turned a ghastly greenish colour.

'How are feeling now Vi?' Olive asked. 'You'll feel better now you've been sick.'

Mother was silent.

After two and a half hours the charabanc struggled to get up Braddons Hill but finally made it and stopped outside an imposing mansion that had once been the Edgemont Hotel, though the last guests had left some time ago. It was a little run down.

We all tumbled out and assembled outside the front door while the driver unloaded the luggage. A man was waiting for us and gave us a list, which indicated which room numbers we were to occupy. We trooped through the front door and up the mosaic-tiled staircase, past some twenty or so stuffed animal heads mounted on the wall, covered in cob webs, their baleful eyes seeming to follow our every move.

'I don't like them!' I shouted out.

'It's a creepy place,' Jean said.

Father told us to be quiet. Somewhere a piano was being played, which made it sound more creepy to me. We were put in a typical en suite hotel room on the first floor. It was sparsely furnished, but had the essentials. There was a large double bed and two single beds. An old table and four chairs were at one end of the room. A bathroom, the first one that I had ever seen, had a huge cast iron bath, a wash basin and a toilet. This was marvellous. Father tried the taps and found that there was only cold water. 'I'll see whether we can get the boiler working so that you can have hot water Vi.'

Everything was covered in a fine layer of dust and a musty smell permeated the room. 'I won't take long to get this place cleaned up,' Mother said, surveying everything.

A large open fireplace was against the inner wall. There were two large French windows, which opened onto a balcony overlooking a magnificent garden, so overgrown with weeds and brambles that it was obvious it had not seen a gardener for a very long time. There weren't any curtains, but the large solid wooden shutters could be used as blackouts. Just under our balcony was a greenhouse.

Auntie Olive and her family were further down the corridor. Father stayed for most of the day to help with settling in. He also managed to fix the boiler. But that evening he had to return home on the charabanc. 'Bye everyone. I shall come to see you as often as I can and Jean, as you are the eldest, look after the children for your mother.'

'Yes Father, I will.' Jean was now nine years old and very sensible.

Mother and Father embraced and kissed and he shook my hand and said, 'You are the man of the family now, so look after your mother.' I was so pleased to be given this role of responsibility at the age of six, although we were sad that he wasn't staying with us.

We didn't get much sleep that night but over the following weeks discovered that the house and garden was a child's paradise, even though a creepy one. The thirteen families which now occupied this defunct hotel had the use of a communal dining room and a kitchen with huge gas ovens. Everything was on a large scale. The cupboards were massive and well stocked with all the cooking utensils that were required. Drawers were full of cutlery, many stamped with the Edgemont Hotel arms. A huge drying room was situated directly above the dining room. Cord had been strung across this room for hanging the damp washed clothes and there was also a drying frame. In the centre of this room was a patchwork of panes of glass, about five feet square, which was cut into the floor and let light into the dismal, dining room below. One of the panes was missing and had been covered with brown paper. Surrounding the skylight there was a wooden bannister rail with spindles, one of which was missing and had been replaced by a piece of rope.

We had many children to play with. Our best friends were Auntie Olive's three children. There were also the three children of Mrs Hindley: Graham, who was fifteen; Thelma, who was about the same age as Jean; and Kenny, the youngest boy. Mrs Boundy had two children, a boy and a girl. Then there were all the children of the other ten families. All in all everyone got along well; occasional arguments broke out over the children for making too much noise or squabbling over nothing much. We children had a wonderful time and Graham Hindley, being the eldest child, kept us under control.

After the first week the children of school age were enrolled in the local schools. Our school was at the lower part of Torquay and we had to descend many stone steps to get there. I liked this school better that the one in Stoke and my teacher was better to me than Miss Cree had been.

One day at school I was feeling ill and was sent home. Jean escorted me and I felt the dire need to go to the lavatory because my stomach was going into painful spasms. Every so often I had to sit on the steps as we ascended them, to avoid messing my pants. 'I can't hold on Jean,' I shouted.

'You'll have to, it's not far now,' she replied. I succeeded in reaching the top step and could see Eagles Cairn just fifty yards down the road. 'Can you hold on till we get there?' Jean asked.

'I'll try my best,' I said, through clenched teeth.

But within two yards of the front door I couldn't control my bowels any longer and diarrhoea gushed down my bare legs into my hobnailed boots. It was such a relief, but now the warm feeling on my skin and the awful stench made me feel terrible and I started to retch. Jean told me to wait and rushed to get Mother. Mother, seeing my predicament, opened the side gate and led me into the garden where she hosed me down, before taking me inside to bathe me and put me to bed. Fortunately, I made a full recovery within a few days.

The gardens were superb for playing in and we built a lookout post so that we could see when enemy aircraft came overhead. We made slits to poke our wooden guns out of, and the rule was that when anyone saw an aeroplane they had to hit two pieces of metal together and shout at the top of their voice, 'Enemy attacking! Enemy attacking!' If we were playing anywhere in the garden we had to run to the lookout post and shoot down the aeroplane. We only ever saw allied planes but pretended that they were the enemy.

Stanley Jones was rather backward with his speech for his age. He made us laugh when he said, 'Enemy ajacket! Enemy ajacket!' The child who laughed the loudest and the longest was Stanley.

We fell out at times and engaged in petty fights. On one occasion Thelma punched Jean on the nose which streamed with blood. We played 'Truth' or 'Dare', though the dare was always the same one. There was a toilet at the end of a long windowless corridor. It was a scary place and the dare was to walk down the corridor in the dark and flush the toilet. I had to do it a couple of times and was terrified because I hated the dark. I nevertheless did it and could feel the hair on the back of my head stand up as my imagination ran riot and I thought that all sorts of ghosts were waiting for me.

In Torquay we didn't suffer the bombings of Plymouth and were able to go on picnics on the beach on Torquay sea front. One day Graham Hindley was in charge of our family and the Joneses and we decided to go to the beach for the day. Although it was too cold for swimming, we played in the rock pools, trying to catch small fish and crabs. We built sand castles and played rounders. We thoroughly enjoyed ourselves, finishing off with our picnic.

On the way back, as we were walking over some seaweed covered steps by the harbour wall, I slipped and fell into the sea, which was about twelve feet deep there. I disappeared under the waves and, not being able to swim, started to drown. Graham, quick as a flash, dived in and grabbed my hair, as I was going under for the second time, and yanked me out. I was coughing and spluttering and then was sick.

Jean said, 'Thank you Graham for saving my brother's life.' She looked at him adoringly. The rest of the children crowded around and patted Graham on the back: 'Well done Graham, you're a hero!'

'I didn't do anything heroic. Anyway he wasn't under for very long.'

Graham carried me as we rushed home to tell Mother what had happened, which upset her. I was shivering with the cold. Graham was still wet through. Mother began to wonder whether coming to Torquay was such a good thing after all. We treated Graham as our hero and all of the girls adored him, especially Jean and Pat. He was very embarrassed at all the attention he was receiving.

The summer months were slipping by and Father and Uncle Bill had been to see us twice. They related to us that the onslaught was continuing in Plymouth and that we were in the best place. However, food in Torquay was in short supply and Mother and the rest of the families found it difficult to manage. Uncle Bill did bring some vegetables for Olive and for Mother which was a great help. They went into the communal kitchen, which was just off the dining room, and made some lovely stew. But it did seem that our family was more accident prone than the others. Jean had gone down to the kitchen to boil a kettle and on the way up had tripped and scalded her arm with the boiling water. Mother heard her screams and rushed to her aid. She liberally smeared her margarine ration over her arms and bound them up with bandages torn from a bed sheet. Jean was sobbing with the pain.

'There, there, now stop crying, you'll be all right,' said Mother soothingly.

'But it hurts Mother.'

Christmas was approaching and some of the mothers said that it would be a good idea to put on a pantomime for all the families. Mother, Olive, Mrs Hindley and Mrs Pope agreed to be on the committee. Mother and Olive would make the costumes and use Olive's sewing machine. One of the mothers had a book of children's stories and thought that *Little Red Riding Hood* would make a good pantomime. It was agreed and Mrs Boundy said she would write the script for it. There were only four main characters: Red Riding Hood, her grandmother, the wolf and the woodsman. The children who would play the parts was to be determined by putting their names into a hat, if they wanted to take part. All the children were assembled and the names were drawn out.

'We need two boys and two girls' said Mrs Pope. 'If it's a girl's part and a boy's name gets picked, we'll carry on until a girl's name comes out. Any questions?'

'What if it's a boy's part and a girl's name gets picked?' shouted Kenny.

'Don't be silly Kenny; it'll work the same as for the girls.'

'I was only asking.'

'Well, ask sensible questions.'

'Right, the first girl's name is for the part of Red Riding Hood. Who would like to pick out that name?'

'I will Mrs Pope,' shouted Maddy.

'Come along then.'

Maddy put her hand in the hat and pulled out a piece of paper. She unravelled it: 'Stanley Jones.'

Everyone laughed. Stanley started to dance around in joy. Mother had tears running down her cheeks and she was holding her stomach.

'Please stop laughing everybody and try to behave.'

Maddy dipped her hand in again: 'Thelma Hindley.'

'Another one Maddy. This will be for the grandmother.'

'Jean Trevail.'

'A boy for the wolf and one for the woodsman,' continued Mrs Pope.

Maddy picked me for the wolf and Graham Hindley for the woodsman. Some of the children were very disappointed that they weren't chosen to play a part, but Mother said that everyone would be in the pantomime if they wanted.

It was to be a very simple panto and rehearsals began the next week. There was a grand piano in the dining room and also a stage at one end. It couldn't have been better. One of the mothers could play piano well, so she agreed to take part.

'I haven't got much sheet music with me, but I'll try my best with music I know by heart. I'm sure I'll manage all right.'

'You'll be fine,' Mrs Pope reassured her.

The script was quickly written by Mrs Boundy and the mothers all agreed to help with costumes and anything else that was needed. Mother said she would ask Father to bring up the costume that I had used for the woodchopper part that I played in the pantomime at Somerset Place School, the previous year. It would be too small for Graham, but another child might fit into it. All the families were excited about the pantomime and it was decided that we would have a party afterwards. We had two rehearsals each week and because the story was quite simplistic the script was easy to manage for all the participants. Father brought up the costume and the wooden axe. He had also made a superb papier mâché wolf's head for me. It had a big mouth with long teeth and staring eyes. He had used the leather tongue from an old pair of boots and painted it red to be the wolf's tongue lolling out of its gaping jaw. I was a bit scared of it, but soon got used to putting it over my head and growling like a wolf. Only those taking part in the pantomime were allowed in the dining room on rehearsal days so that everything would be kept a secret. Olive had made me a wolf's suit from a moth-eaten fur coat, but it looked the part.

As Christmas approached all the costumes were finished and the actors were word perfect. The performance was to be given one week before Christmas Day. Father said that he would be able to come, which pleased me because I wanted him to be proud of my acting.

Everything was ready for the big day. Trestle tables were set up at the back of the dining room and laden down with food that the Mothers had been saving for some time. Wooden chairs were set in rows in front of the stage to accommodate the families and those relatives who would be coming. Someone had rigged up a curtain across the stage. We were as ready as we could be. Mrs Pope was on the stage with us, behind the curtains. We were all very nervous.

'Now remember to speak up and face the audience. Right, now take your places,' Mrs Pope whispered.

The piano started and the curtains were dragged back to reveal the woodland scene with a cottage painted on some cardboard. Red Riding Hood is walking to her granny's cottage carrying a basket, because her granny is ill. I was in the bed because I had already eaten granny and was pretending to be her. Red Riding Hood enters the cottage and greets her granny.

'Oh granny, what big eyes you have,' said Thelma.

'All the better to see you with, my dear,' I shouted.

'And what long nails you have.,'

'Because I lost my nail scissors,' I said. The audience laughed. I was getting very hot in the bed with the fur coat and the wolf's head on.

'And granny, what big teeth you have.'

I shouted, 'All the better to eat you up and I'm going to eat you now.'

I jumped out of bed and started to chase Red Riding Hood around the bed. The little children in the audience were shouting and screaming. The pianist was playing scary music and now I had to chase her off stage and stuff a pillow up my fur coat to pretend that I had eaten her. I came back on stage rubbing my fat tummy, to the boos of the audience. I could see Father in the crowd and was pleased with my performance. Just then I saw Graham approaching with his axe. I hide behind a tree.

'Have you seen that naughty wolf?' he shouts out. He pretends to look everywhere except where I'm hiding.

I'm behind Graham and the children shout out, 'He's behind you!'

'Where?'

'Behind you!'

I had to creep towards Graham slowly. He turns around and strikes me with the axe. I fall to the floor and a cheer goes up. He then drags me behind a white screen where a light projects our silhouettes. He pretends to chop me up.

Red Riding Hood now appears to raucous cheers. Jean comes into view dressed as the granny. Another cheer. Jean and Thelma embrace. Then Graham drags me back on to the stage. The audience boo.

'What shall I do to that naughty old wolf?'

Mrs Pope from the side of the stage shouts, 'Fill his tummy with stones and throw him in the river.'

'What shall we do children?' shouts Graham.

'Fill him with stones!' they all shout.

Graham, Thelma and Jean pretend to fill me with stones and sew up my tummy. They get all the little children who didn't have a part to come on to the stage and lift me to a make-believe river to throw me in. They were all dressed as elves and fairies. A big cheer erupted and the curtain was dragged across. We all took our places on the stage and when the curtain was opened again we bowed to rapturous applause.

Father said afterwards that I was very good. 'You're a natural, Tony.'

* * *

The following week we decorated the family room as best we could with paper chains.

'Father will be coming tomorrow, children,' Mother reminded us.

'Can we meet him at the station please?' begged Jean.

'Yes, can we?' Pat and I asked in unison.

Mother agreed and the next morning we all trooped off to the train station to greet Father. He got off the train hefting a large hessian sack in one hand and a suitcase in the other. He placed them on the platform as we all rushed to greet him. Mother embraced him and they kissed. We sniggered.

'What have you brought, Father?' I asked.

'Just a few things, for Mother. As well as a chicken.'

'Hurrah!'

'Now, who's going to help me with this sack?'

'We will,' we cried.

It took us an hour to struggle up Braddons Hill to Eagles Cairn. Auntie Olive dropped in with a tray of rock buns and a teapot.

'I expect you could all do with a cup of tea and a rock bun.'

'I'm as dry as a bone,' said Father. 'By the way, I saw Bill in the week. He's coming up on a later train.'

Olive poured the tea and said, 'We're all looking forward to seeing him, and the children are very excited.'

'Bill told me an amusing story the other day. When he was on police duty he found two drunken Norwegian sailors sitting on an unexploded bomb at Home Sweet Home Terrace in Cattedown. He told them they should leave immediately. But apparently they just laughed and said, "We have been around the world and now we have found Home Sweet Home, so we cannot leave."'

We all laughed.

After the tea and buns Olive went back to her rooms.

'Right children, up to bed early tonight or Father Christmas won't come.'

We all followed the usual Christmas Eve ritual and went to bed full of expectation, taking some time to get to sleep. In the early hours I awoke and, in the dark, retrieved my pillowcase from the foot of the bed. The noise I made woke Jean and Pat and we whispered to each other in the stillness. When it eventually became light enough to see we showed each other our gifts. I had a model wooden Lancaster bomber painted camouflage, a wooden Tommy gun with a ratchet that made a loud gun noise when turned. I also had a bag of marbles. Jean had a doll and pram. Pat had some colouring books. We took our gifts to show Mother and Father. Baby John had a couple of stuffed animals that Mother had made.

For the Christmas dinner, Father carved the chicken, which tasted delicious, and Mother had hidden some silver threepenny pieces in the pudding. We all seemed to get one. In the afternoon we played our usual indoor games.

Just after tea Father had to leave us to return to his duties in Plymouth. We were all sad.

'Come and see us soon Father, won't you?'

'I'll do my best.'

Amid tears we said our goodbyes once again.

* * *

Early in 1942, on one of his visits, Father brought a little puppy for us to see. It was the loveliest puppy we had ever seen. Someone had sold it to Father in the pub. He was brown and white and jumped up to us licking everything in sight.

'What's he called?' we all chorused.

'I've named him Nikki; he's part Labrador and part something else.'

We had a lovely day playing with the puppy and hated seeing Father go with Nikki, though we looked forward in anticipation to the next time that we would see them.

The weather was very wet in March and the only way to dry the washing was to use the drying room above the dining room. All the families had days allocated to them for using the drying room. Today was Auntie Olive's turn and she was hanging her washing up when my baby brother John wandered into the room. He had left Mother's side when she was occupied with something else.

'Hello John. What are you doing here? Does mummy know that you're here?'

'She down tairs,' baby John replied.

'Well, you stay there until Auntie's finished hanging up the washing and I will take you back to mummy.'

She continued to hang up the clothes as John wandered around the bannister surrounding the skylight. When he got to the rope spindles he pulled one aside and stepped onto the glass pane. Olive saw him out of the corner of her eye and, as she rushed over to lift him out, he stepped on the brown paper that was covering the missing pane of glass and plunged twenty feet to the dining room beneath. She heard his little body hit one of the tables with a sickening thud and, looking through the torn edges of the brown paper, saw him lying there surrounded by the children who had been playing there. She screamed so loudly that everyone heard it and rushed from their rooms.

Mother was quickly on the scene pushing through the children to get to John's lifeless body. Mother gathered him into her arms thinking that he was dead. But John started to whimper and Mother shouted for someone to get a taxi to take him to hospital. Graham rushed up the road to the taxi office and a car came almost immediately. Mother thought that he was going to die.

When they arrived at the hospital, John was taken from her. Some time later a doctor came to her and said, 'Mrs Trevail, I'm afraid that your son has a hairline fracture of his skull and has damaged his right knee.'

'Is he going to die?'

'The next few hours will be critical so we'll just have to wait and see; but I'm hopeful that he'll pull through.'

The Matron phoned Father at the wardens' post; he said he hoped to come as soon as possible.

'I pray to God that he will,' Mother said.

After a few hours Mother was told that John would survive but had to stay in hospital under observation for forty-eight hours. She was so relieved at the news that she sobbed. And within a fortnight John was as right as rain and enjoyed all the fuss that everyone made of him.

* * *

Torquay had endured six enemy attacks up to the beginning of August and Plymouth had not had one. Mother was beginning to feel homesick for the 'res' and wanted to return. Auntie Olive felt the same way. In September we returned to school and there was another attack with high explosive bombs doing a lot of damage.

One Saturday in September the weather was very warm and we children were out, playing around the garden. 'Let's play follow the leader,' Graham said.

Mother saw us walking past the French windows in Indian file following in Graham's footsteps. She opened the windows when she saw Pat on the balustrade. She had tagged along and it wasn't until she was in a dangerous position outside the balustrade that the rest of us saw her. We all shouted at her to stop. Mother rushed out through the French windows to grab her, but it was too late. She lost her balance and went crashing through the roof of the greenhouse. There followed an eerie silence.

Pat was found on her knees, blood gushing from the lacerations the shards of glass had made. She was now screaming in pain and Mother once again was quickly on the scene. There was such a noise that many of the families came rushing to help. Mother took my sister to the family room and for the next hour or so she and Auntie Olive deftly picked out slivers of glass from her knees. Pat was still sobbing from the pain, but was being soothed by us all. When all the glass had been removed, iodine was administered, along with the same bandages that had been used for Jean.

Within a month the cuts had healed, but Pat was left with ugly scars. Mother was getting very agitated about all the accidents and said to Olive, 'This place is jinxed. I want to go home.'

'I do too Violet!'

At the end of September Auntie Ivy came up to see us in the middle of the week, which was very unusual. She had taken sick leave from the Dockyard. Her eyes were red and puffy from crying and looked very ill when she came in.

'What is it Ivy, what's wrong? You look awful,' Mother said.

Ivy rummaged in her handbag and passed a telegram to Mother. Mother's heart missed a beat and, with hands trembling, sunk to the chair and read the bad news.

The War Office regrets to inform you that Private J.H.R. Lambert number 14645579 is missing in action. Presumed dead.

Someone had signed it from the War Office. Mother rushed to Ivy and held her.

'What am I going to do Vi?'

'Perhaps it's a mistake. They do happen you know,' Mother said through her tears.

'They wouldn't have sent it if it wasn't true.'

'But it says that he is missing, and they presume that he has been killed.' But she too felt in her own heart it was true.

'I just feel that he's been killed.' And she broke down sobbing again.

When Father was told he said that he wouldn't believe it until he saw his grave, which wasn't any consolation to Ivy.

We didn't understand what was happening but knew that it was serious. Jean took us outside and said that Mother would explain later. When we realised what the telegram meant we were all heartbroken and cried our hearts out because we loved him so much. Auntie Ivy stayed with us until we returned to Plymouth.

On 3 October a single German aeroplane came over Torquay and we went to the lookout post thinking that it was one of ours. However, no sooner had we entered the lookout than the aeroplane started to machine gun the town and we could see the flames from the gun barrels.

'It's an enemy aircraft,' we all shouted. 'Enemy attacking!' We aimed our wooden guns at it, trying to shoot it down, but to no avail. It eventually flew off.

This was the last straw for Mother and she telephoned Father to come and take us home. He and Uncle Bill arrived; Nikki had been left at the 'res'. We said our goodbyes to our friends, hugging them. Graham kissed Jean on the lips, which made her face go bright red. We struggled with our luggage to the station and boarded the steam train with

Uncle Bill, Auntie Olive and her children. We were sad to leave Eagles Cairn but now were looking forward to seeing the 'res' again and the cottage, but especially Nikki.

Chapter 13

When we arrived at North Road Station in Plymouth we said goodbye to Bill, Olive and the children and caught a bus to Stoke village. We alighted at the top of Ford Hill, right outside Baskervilles the bakers. The bread smelt lovely and we begged Mother to buy us some fancies to have after our tea. Mother went in and bought us some jam doughnuts and a saffron cake. We were delighted.

We trudged the 500 yards or so to the 'res'. Uncle Tom, Rene's husband, was holding Nikki on a leash and, as soon as we came in the gate, he let him off. He rushed at us as we called to him and, with his tail wagging frantically, he jumped up and licked us all over. We were full of glee to see him again.

The neighbours were also at the cottage, waiting to greet us, even though the December weather was wet, dank and utterly miserable. They had got together and put on a wonderful spread for us. Aunt Rene had brought fresh 'bought' cakes and fancies from Baskervilles shop, which we children thought were better than Mother's baking. Mother didn't mention the cakes she had bought and neither did we.

Nan Bryant, a really good friend of Mother, was present too, in her stained pinafore. She seemed to have grown even fatter. Her daughters Sheila and Jill were with her.

As we went through the door which led into the sitting room there was a new wooden structure around one of the alcoves. It surrounded a door.

'What's this then?' Mother asked.

'If you open the door, you'll see,' replied Father. We were all eager and crowing around to see what this door was hiding. 'Move back and let the dog see the rabbit.'

Mother opened the door to reveal a Belfast sink with a tap above it. On the wall at the side was an 'Ascot', a gas operated water heater.

'Oh, John it's wonderful; hot water on tap!' she exclaimed. 'No more having to fill the zinc bath from the copper.' The neighbours clapped.

'I've got a piece of water hosepipe to connect to the end of the hot pipe, so that we can fill the bath directly, and another longer piece that I can empty the bath with.'

'Oh John, you're so clever!' Mother rushed over to Father and planted a big kiss on his lips.

'Ugh!' said we children. But we couldn't wait until Sunday to have our first bath in front of a roaring fire.

We had a lovely tea, the women clucking like mother hens as they caught up on the latest gossip. Auntie Ivy was still grief stricken and could not enter into the joyous occasion and after some little time departed to her home in Park Street. We went to bed utterly worn out, but glad to be back at the 'res'.

Sunday evening came and the bath was brought in and placed in front of the fire. The fireguard, which was made of criss-cross wire with a brass top, was always in place when the fire was lit. (In the winter Mother warmed a bottle of camphorated oil on the guard then rubbed our chests with it to try to prevent us from catching colds.) Father connected the pipe to the heater and turned it on. In moments hot water was flowing into the bath. We all thought that it was marvellous, even though it was a rather slow process. Once the bath was filled, Jean had her bath, followed by me, then Pat and finally John. The water had turned a greyish colour by the time we had all been bathed. It was so cosy in front of the fire. Mother then made us cocoa and we were allowed to listen to the wireless, before we made our way to bed. We were now able to use the sink daily to wash and also to brush our teeth with Gibbs Dentifrice toothpaste, which came in a little aluminium container.

We enrolled again at our old school, Somerset Place School for Boys and Girls. Miss Cree was again my teacher, which made me very unhappy.

In 1943, soon after I had celebrated my seventh birthday, I was taken seriously ill. My temperature was 102 degrees Fahrenheit, my breathing was very rapid and I was delirious. Our family doctor, Dr Morris, was called for and declared, 'He's got double pneumonia with pleurisy and must go to hospital right away.'

The ambulance arrived within half an hour and the attendants wrapped me in a red blanket and carried me out on a stretcher. Mother came with me and on the journey her mind went back to 1939 when Pat, who was then two years old, had had pneumonia, though it hadn't been bad enough to require hospitalisation. Dr Morris had given Mother instructions as to how to apply a kaolin poultice to Pat, which was the recognised treatment. But Mother had misunderstood the instructions and ended up putting the hot poultice directly onto Pat's bare skin, which scalded her and left a nasty scar.

Father saw Dr Morris to the door and asked, 'How ill is the boy, doctor?'

'He's extremely ill indeed, but he'll get the proper treatment in hospital.'

Although I was very ill, I was looked after very well by the doctors and nurses. I began to recover fairly quickly, but some of the treatment was very painful. I had to have injections three or four times a day, alternating between my upper arms and thighs to avoid making them too hard to bear. The other treatment I disliked was their method for clearing my lungs of phlegm. I was rested on a pillow with a towel put over one side of my chest. The nurse would slap my chest with both hands alternately and press to make me cough. This I did and I had to spit into a stainless steel container with a hinged lid. Sometimes I nearly passed out due to hyperventilation. The worst thing I had to endure was the enemas. The nurse placed me on my side and inserted a red rubber tube into my rectum, the other end of which was attached to a white enamel funnel with a blue rim. She held the funnel in one hand and picked up a jug containing soapy water which she poured into the funnel. I was told to hold myself for as long as possible. I then quickly sat on a stainless-steel bedpan and let the floodgates open. What a relief when it was all over.

When I was feeling much better I enjoyed being in the hospital. The men on my ward were very generous in giving me sweets and comics. When I was about to be discharged I was a little sad. Mother and Father had visited me often, and now they came to collect me in Mr Keast's car. I knew I would be starting school again soon, but I had missed so many lessons.

I had only been back at school for two weeks when something awful happened. I had fallen behind the other children in my learning, and on this particular day Miss Cree asked me to spell 'lady'.

I voiced the letters 'l-a-b-y'.

'What did you say?'

I repeated it and she told me to come out to the front of the class and write it on the blackboard. I wrote 'laby' and she screamed at me and snatched the chalk from my hand and wrote it correctly. She then grabbed my ears and as she told me to repeat the letters she banged my head against the blackboard for each letter, making me see stars. My ears were hurt as her long nails tore the skin in furrows behind each ear. I started to cry and she pressed on to my head a white conical hat with the letter 'D' on it and made me stand in the corner of the classroom. She snarled, 'Don't be such a baby, crying like that.' I remained there, crying, for the rest of the lesson, feeling terrible.

When I got home from school that afternoon, Father was in the front of the cottage checking the levels of chlorine. I kept my head down but he called me over to him. 'What's the matter with you then? Been in trouble at school?'

I replied that I had been put in the corner for not being able to spell.

'You'll have to do better then, won't you? You've got chalk on your forehead.'

'I *will* try Father, I promise,' I said, facing him so that he wouldn't see my ears.

'Now go in and tell your Mother.'

As soon as Mother saw me she immediately saw my ears and shouted for Father to come in. 'Look at his ears and this bump on his forehead.'

Father saw the damage and asked, 'Who did that to you?'

'Miss Cree.'

'Well you must have done something terrible for her to do that.'

'I just couldn't spell "lady",' I said , starting to cry again.

'Mother, quickly clean up his ears and I'll take him to see Mr Glanville.'

I did not want to go back to school, but Father was insistent. After my ears were bathed in Dettol and ointment applied, Father marched me back to school. He was very agitated and his rubicund face was getting ever redder. He was muttering under his breath all the way to school. He marched me right up to the headmaster's office and rapped loudly on the door. 'Come in.'

Father opened the door and pulled me into the office. Mr Glanville was sitting at his desk. 'What can I do for you, Mr Trevail?'

Father pointed to my ears, which had started to bleed again, seeping through the ointment.

'How on earth did that happen? Has another pupil done it?' he asked.

'Another pupil? No. Not another child; one of your teachers!'

'Surely not Mr Trevail. You must have made a mistake.'

Father turned to me and said, 'Tony, tell Mr Glanville who did this to you.'

I blurted out that Miss Cree had done it because I couldn't spell a word correctly.

'I'll speak to her this instant.'

'Speak to her? Speak to her? I'll speak to her – with that!' And he unhooked the headmaster's cane off the wall by his table. 'Now, which room is she in?'

'Please Mr Trevail, calm yourself down, that won't solve anything!'

'It will make me feel a lot better.' He turned to leave the room with me. I was scared stiff.

Mr Glanville caught Father's arm and said, 'She's a very ill woman and is due to go into hospital for an operation. Now, please give me the cane.'

'I want to give her a taste of her own medicine, doing that to a boy who has just come out of hospital himself.' I was squirming at the end of Father's arm.

'I beg of you, please calm down and give me back my cane. I promise that I will deal with it.'

Father was beginning to relax a little and reluctantly gave the cane back. 'Well if you promise, I'll leave it to you. But any more of this and I'll go to the School Board and report her.'

'Just leave it with me Mr Trevail.'

Mr Glanville held out his hand to Father and they shook. He also shook my hand, which I just couldn't believe. Father took me home and explained to Mother all that had been said. Mother kept me off school for the rest of the week and, when I returned the following Monday morning, I had a new teacher, Miss Kneebone, who was lovely. I never saw Miss Cree again.

* * *

In the spring of 1943 many camps were set up in Plymouth to accommodate American soldiers. The nearest one to us was set up in Devonport Park, overlooking the Dockyard. We children wanted to see what real Americans were like and asked if we could go. Mother gave us permission and we made our way there. The camp was surrounded with barbed wire and there were lots of tents. We spoke to some of the men through the wire and they gave us sweets and chewing gum. (We would be going again!) There was another American camp in Fore Street, which accommodated African Americans, who were segregated from the whites.

Father was using his inventiveness to collect money for the war effort. In 1941 there had been 'War Weapons Week' and in 1942 there had been 'Warships Week'. Now it was 'Wings for Victory Week' and Father had constructed a two-wheeled cart, to which he attached a dogs harness. On the top of the cart were my models of a Lancaster aeroplane, a grey-painted destroyer and a camouflage-painted Wellington bomber. The cart was draped all over with a Union Jack and colourful bunting. On the back of the cart was a sign which read 'I'm Doing my Bit to Put a Plane in the Sky'. The harness was for Nikki, and he didn't mind one bit. During that week Father took him around Stoke village and the neighbouring district and the people generously gave all that they could afford.

Towards the end of the week, after Father had been out collecting, he was coming up the 'ope' (alley) towards the 'res' when Aunt Rene saw them and called to Nikki. He bounded up to her, over the pavement, tipping the cart over and spilling out all the coins.

'What did you do that for Rene? Where's your sense?' Father shouted.

'I didn't know he would do that,' she replied sheepishly.

'Well perhaps you would like to pick up the money?' he said angrily.

Because of Father's tone of voice Nikki looked downcast and held his tail between his legs. Aunt Rene reluctantly picked up all the money whilst Father looked on, not helping one bit. Rene wasn't Father's favourite person as he thought she was a bit of a gossip and busybody.

'C'mon boy, let's go home.' Nikki's eyes lit up, his head came up and his tail wagged as Father led him home.

We children did our bit for Wings for Victory by pushing an old pram around the area in which was an old gramophone playing 'The Cuckoo Waltz'. It was the only record that we had so we played it over and over again. The best response we got was from Agnes Weston's Royal Sailors Rest. When the sailors heard the music, they opened their windows and showered us with money. We were so pleased with the amount we collected.

By now the Plymouth air raids had ceased and we had slept in our beds, in the cottage, since returning from Eagles Cairn. One of my friends, Peter Aze, was the only boy who wasn't evacuated and had spent the time that we were away in his family's house in Park Street near to Auntie Ivy's house. He related some of the things that had happened while we had been away. His older brother Alan and his friend Edward Dean, both sixteen, had helped to put out incendiaries during the blitz. Another boy called Mick Caton did an invaluable job for the ARP. He was as agile as a monkey and had clambered up drainpipes to get into rooms where incendiary bombs had caught fire. He then threw them down to the men below who extinguished them with buckets of sand. On one particular raid an incendiary had gone through the garage roof of 14 Park Street. 'I'll see to that one.' He was soon up on the roof and, after the men had passed him a couple of buckets of sand, he jumped down to extinguish the bomb. Unfortunately for him this bomb had been fitted with a timed fuse. It exploded in his face, burning it and damaging his eyes. The men quickly got to him after hearing his screams for help. He was rushed to the Royal Eye Infirmary where he stayed for some weeks recovering, before returning to the task as if nothing had happened. He was hailed a hero.

Chapter 14

Auntie Ivy had returned to her job in the dockyard and Mother said, 'She's getting on with her life again, although I feel she is drinking too much.'

'Well she's only trying to get over losing Jack,' Father replied.

'Yes I can see that, but drink never helps anyone,' protested Mother.

'Well you are biased against the demon drink; don't say you're not.'

Ivy's friend Ruby encouraged her to start enjoying life again. 'Come on Ivy, you can't grieve for Jack for the rest of your life.'

'I just feel it's not right to be enjoying myself when I think of what Jack has been through.'

Ruby kept up her encouragement for a long time. 'Listen Ivy, I've heard that the black GIs go to the Paramount Dance Hall on Saturdays. You know, the one in Union Street. They're great at jitterbugging. Shall we go?'

'Ruby, that's the biggest dive in Plymouth and I wouldn't be seen dead there.'

'Oh stop it Ivy. Put your glad rags on and come with me, next Saturday, please.'

'I'll think about it, but no promises.' Ruby smiled to herself, knowing that her persistence had paid off.

Saturday came and the two of them, looking glamorous, made their way up the stone steps which led up to the Paramount. Many drunken sailors had tumbled down these steps. They heard the music which was getting louder with each step they took. They looked at each other and their hearts started racing. They passed their coats to the cloakroom attendant and took their tickets.

'Let's sit at a table Ruby.' They made their way through the crowd to a spare table and sat down. A five-piece band were on a raised stage and they were very good.

'I'll go up to the bar and get us some drinks,' said Ruby.

Ivy looked around. The smell of tobacco smoke, alcohol and cheap scent filled the room. Ivy's eyes began to smart. She caught sight of a group of African Americans leaning against the bar. There were also British soldiers and a few sailors. Ivy had never seen a black man before, but she liked what she saw.

Ruby came back with the drinks. 'I like the look of those American soldiers,' she said, 'they're so different to our boys; their uniforms are so smart.'

The band struck up a fast number and some of the GIs took partners and started to jitterbug. Ruby and Ivy sat with their eyes glued to the dancers. 'It's marvellous Ivy. I wonder if we'll get asked,' Ruby said.

The MC announced another number and two GIs made their way towards the two girls. 'Look out Ruby, here they come.'

Both men were tall and extremely handsome. 'Hi there pretty missies. Could we have the honour of this dance?'

'We can't jitterbug, can we Ruby?' Ivy tentatively said.

'We could try, Ivy,' replied Ruby.

'I could teach you. It's easy peasy. By the way my name is Noah. I'm from Georgia, USA. We are in the SOS.'

'What does that stand for?' asked Ivy.

'It's Services of Supply. I'll tell you all about it later, if you will dance with me.'

'I'm Ivy and this is my friend Ruby.'

Noah said, 'May I introduce my buddy Charles?'

'Charmed, I'm sure,' replied Ruby, who shook Charles's hand.

Charles led Ruby onto the dance floor and Noah held out his hand to Ivy. She reluctantly accepted and took her place. The music was lively and the girls started jitterbugging. They soon got the hang of it and before long even Ivy was laughing and really enjoying it. It was very strenuous though. When the dance ended the soldiers escorted them back to their table. They were all hot and thirsty. 'Drinks ladies?' Charles enquired.

'We'd like a pink gin each, please,' replied Ruby.

'Pink gins it is.' Charles made his way to the bar and Noah sat next to Ivy. Charles brought the drinks back and sat down. They clinked glasses. Ruby said, 'Bottoms up!'

'Never heard that one before,' Noah replied.

Ivy looked at Noah and thought that he was very handsome. He smelt divine, of fresh soap or men's cologne. Ivy was thirsty and downed her drink quickly. It went straight to her head and she felt a little squiffy. They danced again and drank a little more. Ivy was having a really good time. The girls were being thrown all over the place. The jitterbugging was hectic, but they loved it. Thoughts of Jack didn't enter her head. She drank more and was feeling very happy.

Just before midnight a waltz was announced and Ruby, Ivy and their partners took to the floor for the last time. Noah was dancing far too close for Ivy's liking and she pulled away, but he pulled her back, resting his cheek on hers. Her cheek burned, but she left it there. The dance ended and he tried to kiss her on the lips, but she turned her head and he kissed her on the cheek. 'Aw, come on honey, just one kiss.'

'I hardly know you,' she replied.

'Can I see you home, Ivy?'

'I'm not sure what Ruby is doing.' She saw Ruby with her arms around Charles and guessed that she would be going with him. 'I'll see you soon Ruby. Look after yourself.'

'Of course I will.'

Charles turned to Ivy and said, 'You'll be OK with Noah, he'll see you safely home.'

'Well if you're sure.'

Noah and Ivy made their way to the taxi rank. Ivy felt a little unsteady on her feet as the cold night air cooled her face. They boarded the taxi. 'Where to my luvver?' the driver enquired.

'The top of Ford Hill in Stoke please,' Ivy replied.

When they arrived, Noah paid the driver and turned to her and said, 'I'll walk you to your home, pretty Ivy.' But Ivy didn't want anyone to see her with a black American, so she said, 'You can walk me to the bottom of the ope, but no further.'

The night was clear as they made their way unsteadily along Molesworth Road. They had only gone about twenty yards when the sirens sounded; then they heard enemy aircraft droning in the night sky, not too far away.

'Quick, there's a shelter just around the corner,' Ivy said. He grabbed her hand and dragged her to the shelter. They rushed inside. Bombs were beginning to crump nearby. It was pitch black inside the shelter and it smelt of urine. 'I'm afraid,' she said shakily.

'Don't worry, you're safe with me. Didn't you hear what Charles said?' He felt for her in the blackness and pulled her to him in a strong embrace.

'What do you think you're doing?' she exclaimed. Her head was still spinning a little and she felt sick. He tried to kiss her on the lips. 'Please stop it. I don't want you to.'

'C'mon, all the girls say that, but they don't mean it,' he retorted. The noise was deafening outside and the bombs seemed to be very close. Now and again they felt the draught of the blast, as it came in the doorway. He started pawing at her clothes and dragged her down onto the wooden slats that covered the wet floor of the shelter. He tried to undo the buttons on her blouse; she screamed, but it was lost in the cacophony of the noise outside. She scratched his face, which inflamed him. 'A little spitfire, eh? I love them like that.'

'Get off me,' she pleaded. He punched her in the face and she lost consciousness.

When she started to come round, he was still raping her. Then he got up and ran from the shelter. The all clear sounded. But she lay there, in the filth and the smell, for a very long time before eventually staggering to her feet and making her way back to her flat.

She let herself in and tore her clothes off. She ran a bath of cold water; there wasn't any hot. She felt numb and violated. She scrubbed herself raw, with a floor scrubber, trying to get rid of the smell of him and his filth.

She couldn't remember how long she'd sat in the bath but her lips had turned blue and she couldn't stop her teeth chattering. Then she got into bed and waited for the dawn.

Father was awakened by the noise of the porch bell being rung. 'Who can that be at this time in the morning?' He jumped out of bed and looked out of the window. 'It's your sister Ivy. What does she want at this hour on a Sunday morning?'

Mother was out of bed in an instant, shrugging on her dressing gown. 'I'm coming Ivy!' she shouted. When she opened the door, Ivy slumped into her arms. 'There, there, come inside and sit down. I'll put the kettle on and make us all a nice cup of tea.'

Ivy started to sob; the tears coursing down her face. Father was down by this time. Mother asked, 'Ivy, what is it? Tell us what's happened.'

Ivy related all that had taken place the night before, every few minutes breaking down unable to speak. Father was livid. 'I'm reporting this to the police, as soon as they open. In fact I'll go to the police box now and telephone for someone to come.' He was already dressed.

'Have your tea first and then go,' said Mother.

'It's all my fault; I should never have gone with Ruby in the first place.' They sipped their tea then Father left.

Mother comforted Ivy as best she could. 'You'd better stay with us until this is sorted .'

'Vi, I feel so violated and dirty. He was so nice at first, but then he seemed to turn into an animal.' Violet pulled Ivy to her breast and comforted her.

Father came back fifteen minutes later. 'The police will be here to take a statement from you Ivy.'

'Oh, what have I done?' Ivy wailed.

'You did nothing. It was that horrible black man,' Mother said.

Two plain-clothes detectives arrived an hour later. They introduced themselves and asked if Mother and Father would go into the sitting room while they interviewed Ivy. After she had given her statement, the detectives said that they would be in touch.

Later that day Father contacted Ruby. She was appalled at what she heard and said that Charles had been a perfect gentleman and that she had arranged to see him again. Ruby was so upset at what had happened and felt guilty about it because she had encouraged her friend to accompany her to the dance.

Over the following weeks Ivy stayed at our cottage. We children wondered why she was living with us as we were so cramped; but we weren't told the reason of course. Meanwhile the detectives had been to the army camp and spoken to the colonel in charge. There were two soldiers with the name Noah, so Ivy was asked if she would accompany them to the camp to pick him out. She was reluctant to go but was assured that he would not see her. So she agreed and went, with Mother supporting her.

The two soldiers were being held in a cell together. Ivy looked through a spyhole in the door and froze as she recognised one of them as her assailant. She indicated this to the officer. The colonel said to the detectives and Ivy, 'This is a military matter and we'll deal with it by court martial. I'm sorry that you have suffered so much at the hand of one of my men, but I promise you that justice will be done.'

Ivy asked tremulously, 'Will I have to give evidence?'

'Yes, I'm afraid you will.'

Mother interjected, 'Listen Ivy, that animal needs to be tried for what he did to you. You have to give evidence.'

The court martial duly arrived and Ivy gave her evidence. Her assailant was found guilty by a majority decision and sentenced to ten years hard labour. He was to be shipped back to a stockade in America. Ivy and Mother returned to the 'res' satisfied with the outcome. But no one was to know the legacy he had bestowed on Ivy.

Chapter 15

On the night of Saturday 12 June 1943 the air-raid siren sounded just after midnight. We all awoke quickly and rushed down to the shelter and slammed the door shut. Soon after Pathfinder enemy aircraft dropped flares across Plymouth which lit the city up as if it were broad daylight. This was to assist the twenty German bombers that followed. We heard the all too familiar sound of the bombs exploding and we could hear the Bofors gun pounding away in the back lane. Tracer bullets from the gun emplacements tore into the night chasing the bombers. Father was with the wardens observing the action just outside the ARP shelter. A jubilant shout arose, 'He's been hit! He's been hit!'

Mother tentatively opened the shelter door and shouted to Father who came back to tell us that a German bomber had been hit and was on fire. Jean and I rushed past Mother to get a look at the action. There in the night sky, searchlights following its every turn, a plane was on fire. What a sight it made as it headed towards Dartmoor. Father came over and held me close. But as we watched, the plane slowly made a U-turn and started to head straight towards us, descending all the time, belching out smoke and flames. 'Get in the shelter quick!' Father shouted. We rushed back inside and Mother shut the door. Moments later we heard the plane as it roared overhead at only 100 feet. Then there was a huge explosion as it crashed nearby.

Father with some of the wardens rushed out in the direction of the crash to see what could be done. The plane had come down in the garden of a house used by the Women's Royal Naval Service in Penlee Way, who operated a searchlight close by. Rene Lamble who was an ARP warden was one of those who ran to the wreck. She suffered quite badly with arthritis in her legs and was trailing behind the other wardens. When she got to the scene she went into the garden where bullets were exploding from the intense heat of the remains of the bomber. 'Get out of there Rene! You'll get your head shot off!' Father shouted. Despite her arthritis, she proceeded to break the hundred metre sprint record as she ran away.

The plane was a Junkers 88, and all but one of the aircrew died in the crash. One bailed out too late and hit the trees surrounding the garden, which shredded his body to pieces. RAF personnel, the local police as well as the Auxiliary Fire Service (AFS) were quickly on the scene to cordon it off and put out the fires. Father came back in the early hours of the morning and told us what had happened. As he spoke my only thought was that there would be lots of shrapnel there and I would have to get some.

On Sunday morning after breakfast Mother was getting us ready for Sunday School. We attended Belmont Methodist Church, not too far from the cottage. Jean, Pat and I went fairly regularly and we had even signed the pledge not to drink alcoholic beverages. I had determined to get away from Jean and avoid Sunday School at the first possible moment. Mother had dressed me in my best suit, which was of a light brown serge. The trousers came down to just under my knees where they met my long stockings. I wore my best boots and these had cardboard soles because leather was in short supply. I was fidgeting and Mother said, 'For goodness sake keep still Tony, you've never been in a hurry to get to Sunday School before. What's wrong with you?'

I just couldn't wait to get to the wreckage site. As soon as we got to the bottom of the lane I tugged my hand free and ran as fast as I could towards Penlee Way. 'Tony, where are you going? I'll tell Father when I get home.'

'I'm going to get some shrapnel from the German plane.'

As I rounded the corner I met my friend Gerald Burridge, who had the same idea as me. We could smell the burnt oil and other burning smells as we neared the site of the crash. Unfortunately most of the area was cordoned off and there were policemen making sure that no one got too close. RAF personnel were sifting through the smouldering remains and there were many spectators milling around. 'We won't get any shrapnel here,' Gerald said.

We then spotted a green silk parachute caught in a tree and the body of the airman, minus a leg, in the harness. Both Gerald and I felt sick. The AFS had a ladder against the tree and were trying to get the man and the parachute down. 'That's the German airman that my Father told us about last night ,' I said.

Underneath the tree we saw a heap of sand stained dark red, with an airman's boot sticking out of it. We knew that the airman's leg must be buried underneath. 'Ugh!' we exclaimed.

A policeman told us to move on. So we went to a section of the garden hedge that was still intact and where some men were looking over to see what was happening in the garden. We were too small to see over so we asked a man to lift us up to see and he placed us on top of the wall so that we could look over the hedge. We had to strain on tiptoes but could just make out that the garden was devoid of any shrubbery and instead was filled with the still smouldering remains of the aircraft. It was recognisable as a plane but not as a Junkers 88. My heart gave a jump as I saw a swastika, which was clearly visible. I had only ever seen pictures of it before.

Lots of RAF men in overalls were sifting through the wreckage and the smell of burnt oil was awful, which made my stomach turn. An RAF photographer was recording the scene and, as we were looking about, he pointed the camera in our direction. 'That man just took our photo, Gerald.'

'I don't think he was taking our photo, Tony.'

'Well I bet you a piece of shrapnel we're in it because he pointed his camera at us.'

We were lifted back down again and we wandered around the corner where there were only a few people. I saw a small hole halfway up in the hedge and thought that it would be a way to get in and obtain some shrapnel. Gerald helped me up and adroitly I started squirming through the hedge. But after only a couple of feet I was dragged back out by a large policeman who placed me on the pavement. I was so scared that I wet my trousers, my best Sunday trousers. Gerald had disappeared and the policeman, seeing my predicament, laconically told me to go home immediately and not to come back. I stammered, 'Yes sir, I will,' then ran up the road wet and dirty.

Gerald was waiting for me further on. 'Look at your clothes, they're covered in mud. And you smell of piddle. You'll get it when you go home.' I knew that I would be in for a hiding and would just have to face it.

Mother gave me a good tickling with the cane when I arrived home, for not going to Sunday School and for ruining my Sunday clothes. But the real ignominy of it all was my failure to get one piece of shrapnel.

On Monday 14 June Father was reading the local paper, *The Western Morning News*, when he shouted to me, 'Tony come here! Your picture is in the paper.' And there was the picture of the wreck with Gerald and me looking over the hedge. I was vindicated! We all excitedly looked over Father's shoulder as he read out the article to us.

German raiders paid a high price for a sharp attack, which they made on a South West Coast town during Saturday night. Out of a force, four are believed to have been shot down. One of these machines crashed to its destruction in a residential district of the town, and was burnt out, together with a number of the crew.

'You're famous Tony, no one in this family has had their picture in the paper before. We'll have to cut it out and frame it to hang on the wall,' Father said sardonically. I felt really proud and Mother cut out the photograph. It never did get framed and eventually was lost.

Later that day I was sent home from school after vomiting in the playground. This was due to the awful smell from the previous day, which I couldn't get out of my mind, as well as to the sights of that day. However, a few days later, Peter Aze showed us a piece of fuel pipe from the plane, which someone had given him, and which made all the boys very envious. The dead German airmen were buried in unmarked graves at Weston Mill Cemetery.

Chapter 16

The raids ceased again and Father thought that it would be safe to take us to the beach on Sundays if the weather was good. Mother got up at 6 a.m. to make pasties, which were wrapped in towels to keep them hot and then placed into biscuit tins. This kept them very warm and we later enjoyed them immensely.

We usually met up with Father's relatives and made up a party of as many as twenty at times. The regulars were Uncle Ed Elford, his wife Lucy and my cousin Ted; Charlie and Amanda Brock and their son Colin; and Ivy and Tom Lacy and their two daughters. Getting to the beach at Bovisand was difficult. We caught a bus from Stoke village to Phoenix Wharf at the Barbican and then took a ferry to Turnchapel. From there we walked uphill for two miles and then another quarter of a mile to the beach. We all had to carry something to help, even the very young children. Father took a kettle, bottles of water and a blowlamp for boiling water to make tea. As we passed Fort Stamford we shouted into an opening that echoed back to us. We always had a wonderful time on the beach, splashing in the waves and delving into rockpools for crabs and small fish. Father would take me into the sea. I couldn't swim but would put my arms around his neck and he swam with me holding on. At the end of the day, we all trudged up the steep path to a grassy knoll where we had our tea, exhausted but very cheerful.

On some occasions Father paid Mr Keast to take us in his large green Austin 16 motor car, which we children thought very posh. Mr Keast was old and 'doddery' and wore thick-rimmed glasses that were always covered in grease. He had a ramshackle garage repair business at the back of our cottage.

Mr Legge worked with him and they used to pee in an old tin can. Whenever I was allowed to go and see what car they were working on, there was always an awful smell of stale urine from the rusty tin can. Mr Keast always had a cigarette dangling from the side of his mouth and a dewdrop dangling from his nose. But Mother lost confidence in him when he drove through a red traffic light on the way back from the beach and, although we got through unscathed, we never went by car again.

One warm Saturday in July 1943, Jean took us to Victoria Park for the day. We played on the swings and then we met some other children there and a boy gave Jean a Will's Woodbine cigarette, which he lit with a match from a packet of Swan Vestas. She took a puff and passed it around to us for a puff each. 'Don't dare say anything to Mother when we get home. All promise.' We all promised. But when we got home, the first thing that Pat said to Mother was, 'Smell our breath. We haven't been smoking.' We all received the tickler for that. So Pat wasn't very popular with us for a while.

To make ends meet Mother had taken in a lodger called Bert Hammet whose wife and son Billy had not returned from evacuation. Bert was in the Home Guard and was very proud when he wore his uniform, especially his boots which were buffed up to a high shine. One day I was with some of my friends in the shelter further down the ope, where Auntie Ivy had been raped. We were smoking cigarettes. Father had been peeping over the wall and saw us. He let us get on with it, guessing what the consequences would be. After a short while I felt very ill and with my face a strange green colour ran up to the cottage. 'What's wrong Tony? You're not looking too good.' I just ran past him and got inside the front door, where I was violently sick into Uncle Bert's shiny boots. He had just cleaned them and shouted in rage and carried them out on a shovel to the tap by the washhouse. Mother cleaned me up and took me to bed. Uncle Bert asked Father who was going to clean them. 'Well Tony was sick in them, so he should clean them.' Mother interjected and said that I was too ill to do it. Uncle Bert said that Father had better clean them, as he was on duty in one hour and needed them. Father reluctantly washed them out and made an attempt at drying them. But he started retching as he smelt the vomit and vowed in his mind that I would pay for it. Uncle Bert was forced to wear the boots on parade and, although they looked quite acceptable, they were very damp and uncomfortable. He left soon after that.

I was made to sweep the patch in front of the cottage every Saturday morning. I usually took about two hours, and I had to wet it down because of the dust that rose. I had just finished this onerous task one Saturday and, as it was a warm summer day, went up the forbidden path to the top of the 'res' to relax in the long grass. After an hour of lying in the sun I decided to return by another route. This was by way of the three pipes that the AFS used to fill their tenders with water. I sat astride the middle pipe, which was a little smaller in diameter than the two outer pipes. I gingerly made my way down, sliding along on my bottom, legs dangling on either side. I kept a sharp lookout for Mother or Father because, if I was caught, I knew I would catch it in the neck severely (as it happened I did catch it in the neck by my own doing). As I reached the lowest point, which was by the outside wall, I tried to squeeze down between the middle and outer pipes. My body just got through but my ears stopped my head from passing further. My feet were about six inches off the ground and I supported my weight with a hand around the pipes. But my hands couldn't get a firm hold because of the size of the large pipes and I was hanging by my head, which was very painful. My strength was being sapped and I shouted at the top of my voice for Mother.

Mother was at the sewing machine making me a jerkin from an old plaid skirt, singing along to Anne Shelton's 'Taking a Chance on Love' on the wireless, and didn't hear me shouting. She said later that it was intuition that made her look out of the window and see me dangling by my head. My legs were jerking and my face was turning a shade of purple; my arms hung loosely by my sides. Her blood nearly froze in her veins, but, in a flash, she was bounding down to save me. 'Hang on Tony, I'm coming.'

But I didn't hear a thing because I was slipping into unconsciousness, though I do remember coming around as she was pushing me up through the pipes and carrying me up to the cottage. 'What's happened?' I spluttered. Then I remembered. 'Please don't tell Father.'

'You'll be the death of me. What have I told you about climbing on those pipes?'

'I promise I won't do it again.'

Mother kept her promise and didn't tell Father. However, some years later someone in the family said, 'Remember when Tony got his head stuck in the pipes?' And it all came out, though by now I was too old to get a hiding.

Mother was always thinking up new ways of making ends meet and she took a part-time job as a 'clippie' (conductor) on the buses. Unfortunately, when climbing the stairs to the top deck to collect the fares and clip the tickets, she frequently hit her shins as the bus jolted along. So that job didn't last long. But, as fate would have it, another took its place soon after.

We children still visited the Americans in Devonport Park, speaking to them through the barbed wire which surrounded the camp. Adults were interested as well as we children and some said that the barbed wire was to keep the 'yanks' in and not to keep the civilians out. The main reason for us going regularly to speak to them was that they were always giving us the things that we didn't get in the way of sweets and chocolate. They gave us chewing gum, Lifesaver sweets that were in the shape of lifebelts, Hershey bars and sometimes they fed us ice cream from a large enamel bowl, using one spoon for us all, which wasn't at all hygienic but we didn't mind at all. We admired them greatly and thought that they knew all the American film stars like Roy Rogers, Bud Abbot and Lou Costello and the like. They played us along but we liked them immensely.

One day the four of us were there and Jean was talking to a particularly nice 'yank' called Leroy, whom we had talked to before on many occasions. 'Say, young missy, would your mother launder some clothes for me? Cos I ain't no great shakes at it?'

Jean didn't understand what he had meant, so he explained that it was washing clothes. 'My mother is good at washing clothes, look at Tony's shirt,' she explained. My shirt was as white as virgin snow, as I had not had enough time to get it dirty.

'If she'll do it, I'll pay her well,' he said.

Mother agreed and she took in washing for Leroy. He was so pleased that he paid her very well. This service grew from one man to several. Jean and I had to collect the dirty washing and return it clean and expertly laundered. We carried a large wicker basket with a handle at each end, which was very heavy for us, but Mother also paid us, so it was worth the effort. This job continued until the Americans left Plymouth in 1944.

The Americans weren't the only foreigners in Plymouth. There was a contingent of Polish sailors billeted at a large house in Wingfield Villas that was not too far from the 'res'. Mother was hanging out some washing one day when she heard some strange singing coming from the direction of the back lane. She looked over the wall and saw two very drunk Polish sailors lurching along. They saw her looking over and whistled and called out in an obstreperous way. She grabbed John and went into the cottage and locked the door, very frightened. Then she went upstairs and peeked out of the window, making sure that she couldn't be seen.

The sailors reached the wall by the cottage and saw the small chicken run where Father had a few chickens. They clambered over the wall and went into the run amid much squawking from the chickens and drunken laughter from them. Mother kept John quiet so that they wouldn't hear him. They grabbed a couple of chickens and staggered up to the porch of the cottage where they rang the bell. But she kept still and prayed that they would leave. After a few minutes, holding the flapping chickens by their legs, they staggered off. However, they had left the door of the chicken run open so that the other chickens came out and roamed all over the front gardens.

Mother waited for ten minutes and then spent another hour herding the rest of the absconding chickens into the run. Father was livid when she told him, and he immediately contacted the officer in charge, who apologised profusely. He gave Father some produce to make up for the loss of the chickens.

* * *

Auntie Ivy was off work for three weeks recovering from her horrific ordeal. Ruby tried her best to comfort her when she made time to visit. She returned to her job in the dockyard and settled back into the routine. But not too long after she began to feel unwell and was forced to take more time off. Mother, despite all the work she had to do for our family, made up a bed for her in our sitting room in order to look after her. But Ivy became so ill that Mother called for Dr Morris.

'What seems to be the trouble, Mrs Lambert?'

'I've a strange rash on my body, even on the soles of my feet, and I've been suffering from terrible headaches.'

'Let's have a look at you shall we?'

Mother stood in the background as he did his examination.

'I'll give you something for the rash and I'll come and see you in a few days. Would you see me to the gate, Mrs Trevail?' Mother escorted him and he said with concern in his voice, 'I've something to tell you that I don't want your sister to hear.'

Mother felt anxious. 'Do you know what venereal disease is?'

'I have an idea.' She had seen notices posted up in the public lavatories around Plymouth.

'Your sister has a particularly virulent venereal disease I believe; it's the first stage of syphilis.'

Mother was dumbfounded and spluttered, 'Yes and I know who gave that to her. She was raped by a black American.'

'Oh dear, I'm so sorry to hear that. Did he get caught and dealt with?'

'Yes, he was sentenced for a long time in a stockade in America.'

'Where's Mr Lambert?'

'I'm afraid that he was killed in Burma.'

'I am so sorry.'

'Will my sister die?'

'I'll come and give her injections, but I can't guarantee anything. It's a virulent disease, and people can die from it.'

'Oh no! I don't want her to die.'

'Now this is what you'll have to do. You must be very careful with hygiene. Keep everything your sister uses separate from the rest of the family: towels, cutlery, flannels, everything. This is a highly contagious disease.'

Mother assured him that she would see to it. Dr Morris left and Mother stayed by the front gate for a long time, trying to come to terms with the terrible news of her sister possibly dying. This on top of all the horrible things that had happened: the blitz, Jack's death, the evacuation and all the problems there, and now her sister. She could not contain herself and the tears flooded down her cheeks as she slumped onto the garden border.

When Father came in, Mother took him into the porch and told him all that Dr Morris had said. 'I'm not very happy that she's here. We could all catch it.'

'How can you be so callous? She's my sister and I've promised to look after her. She's very ill and she doesn't know it.' Father saw the determination in her face and reluctantly agreed.

Over the following months Dr Morris came regularly and administered injections of bismuth. Her rashes were beginning to ooze pus and the task of looking after her was becoming intolerable for Mother and Jean, who was also helping her. Dr Morris said that she was getting too ill and would have to be admitted to the City Hospital. Ivy asked mother if the doctor had told her what was wrong with her. But she had to lie and say that she didn't know, but that hospital was the best place to get well, because they could look after her better than she could. Dr Morris arranged for her to be taken by ambulance. Father was very relieved for Mother, but more so for himself. He was afraid of catching any sort of disease.

Chapter 17

The summer of 1943 came and we broke up for the six weeks school holidays. On sunny days most of our friends played in Cundy's field. We also played in St. Aubyns Cemetery, which was overgrown and not used. We were frightened of a man who was always walking around the cemetery, whom we called 'Lofty' because he was very tall. He dragged his foot as he walked and we used to shout to him; but when he came towards us we ran off scared stiff. The story was that he had lost his wife which had 'turned his mind' and that he visited her grave everyday.

All the children that had been evacuated had now returned, and so we were able to have really good fun. My circle of friends these days consisted of Gerald Burridge (my best pal), Peter Aze, Peter Carlisle, Bernard Bannister and Raymond Smith (who was very fat and had the ability of sticking his tongue right up his nostrils). We laughed our heads off when he performed this feat. There was also Raymond Banks, Stuart Herring, Graham Steer (he couldn't sound his Rs and always wanted to be Woy Wogers the cowboy, when we played cowboys and Indians) and David Wales, Peter Aze's cousin. Jean and Pat's friends were Sheila Bryant, Jill Bryant, Maureen Mellett (the boys' sweetheart), Pat Olver, Margaret Luscombe and Dona Wales.

The fields were still a wonderful place for playing in and we built camps in the barns using bales of straw, which was very dangerous because we used candles to light our way, not realising the potential danger that we were in. We had rigged up a swing on one of the oak trees, twenty feet above the ground. Once someone fell off the rope and broke an arm, but that was the only accident. We made bows and arrows and catapults; and we smoked acorn pipes using dried leaves as tobacco.

Surrounding the fields was a black iron-railing fence with sharp spikes at the top. We sometimes climbed on this fence and jumped down into the fields, as a short cut. One day Stuart Herring missed his footing and became impaled through the thigh. He couldn't move and shouted out in pain. Fortunately Victor Bryant, Nan Bryant's eldest son, had been walking his greyhound in the fields and was able to lift him off the railings. But his wound took months to heal up.

Nikki our dog came everywhere with us and all the children loved him. Father really loved his dog, but was strict with him. And Nikki adored his master.

Father told us children that we were winning the war in Europe and that we were fairly safe in Plymouth. However, on 12 August 1943, there was another raid. It was a warm night so we all rushed to the shelter in our pyjamas and as usual stayed the night. Father had been busy with the other wardens dealing with incendiaries. Forty people lost their lives that night. Auntie Ivy, who was the only patient in a ward that caught fire, was unable to shout because of the condition of her throat, but fortunately the nursing staff got her to safety.

Usually Mother took Jean with her when she visited Auntie Ivy, but on one occasion she asked me if I would like to go. When we arrived a porter showed us to the ward where she had been moved to after the fire. I looked for her but couldn't recognise anyone. 'She's not here Mother!'

Mother pointed down the ward to a bed. 'There she is.'

I looked to where she was pointing and only saw an old woman who was very skinny, with most of her hair missing. 'That's not my Auntie Ivy, she's young not old.'

'Shush! Don't talk so loud, you'll disturb the other patients. It is Auntie Ivy and she is very, very ill.' I was shocked, but when we approached the bed I could see that indeed it was her.

Mother embraced Ivy and her eyes welled up with tears. 'I've brought Tony to see you for a change, Ivy.'

Auntie Ivy held out her hand to me but I was afraid to take it. 'I'm so glad you've come to see me Tony. I've missed you and Pat and John.' She spoke in a raspy low voice, not at all like my Auntie. 'Vi, the sister's told me what I'm suffering with and that I probably won't recover from it.'

'Oh Ivy, don't say that. You'll be all right.'

'No Vi, I won't,' she rasped. 'Oh Vi, I do miss Jack so much. He was a lovely husband and didn't deserve to die.'

'Yes Ivy, he was. Do you remember the things that he used to get up to? Remember when he smuggled out those army blankets around his waist then walked out through the barrack gates as brash and confident as you like?'

'I remember that well,' Ivy said. 'He was always an incorrigible rogue.'

'He gave us two of those blankets and they were a godsend,' replied Violet.

Ivy made a weak croaky laugh. 'I'll never forget the first time he took Ruby and me home from the Corn Exchange. I can see Ruby in that sidecar, terrified and screaming for Jack to slow down. I laughed my head off.'

Mother and Ivy continued to talk about Jack and what a character he had been. Mother said later that she thought Ivy was beginning to lose her memory on account of some of the things that she said. But Ivy never mentioned the day she was raped. Apparently she had found out that she had syphilis soon after she was admitted. As Mother was talking she kept falling asleep. I didn't like the horrible smell of disinfectant.

We said goodbye after an hour and on the way out the matron called Mother aside and said in a hushed tone, 'I'm afraid Ivy is getting a little worse, Mrs Trevail. Sometimes patients with this disease go on for months, even years. It's hard to determine. Each patient is different.'

I could see that Mother was very upset. She had to sit down. 'I suppose I knew that,' she replied.

'We'll do everything in our power to make her as comfortable as possible,' the matron continued.

Mother thanked her and we caught the bus back home. I told Mother that I never wanted to go to the hospital again, because the smell made me feel sick. That evening, after our tea, Mother and Father told us all that Auntie Ivy was very ill. We all clung to each other and wept.

As the summer holidays were coming to an end, none of us was looking forward to returning to school. A week before, just after we had finished our tea, Father asked us, 'Has anyone seen Nikki? He's usually home by now.'

'No Father, but he was in the fields earlier,' I said. 'He was over by the quarry.

'Come on, we'll all look for him,' father said.

We went into the fields, calling his name, 'Nikki! Nikki! Come on boy. Where are you?' We whistled as well and hoped that he would soon respond, barking or bounding up to us. Father decided to go up on the reservoir because it afforded a good view. Jean and I were over by the quarry, where I had last seen him, and Mother was with Pat and John near the cemetery wall. Suddenly Father shouted, 'I've spotted him. He's lying down over in the long grass by the edge of the quarry, near you Jean.'

We ran to where Father was pointing and soon found him, lying down whimpering. As we got near he bared his teeth at us and growled; something he had never done before to us. Father had come down and Mother was also making her way to where he was. When Father reached his beloved dog he said quietly, 'Hello old boy. What's the matter then?' Nikki raised his head and looked at Father with sorrowful eyes and whimpered. He was drooling and his muscles were twitching uncontrollably. Father swept him up into his arms and said, 'I think he's been poisoned.' We headed back to the cottage.

'What can we do?' Mother asked.

'Run on ahead and get a jug of water with plenty of salt in it. We'll try to make him sick.'

I stayed with Father while the rest ran home. When we got there, Mother was still scraping salt from the block she had into an enamel jug. Father was out of breath as we arrived on the scene. Nikki's eyes were closed and he was really floppy in Father's arms. Father gently laid him down on the warm brown flagstones in front of the cottage and opened his jaw and started to pour the salt water down his throat, to make him vomit.

By now Father was getting desperate, as there was little response from Nikki. We were all shouting, 'Come on Nikki, you can do it! Be sick! Don't give up!'

But all the encouragement was in vain. He gave a little shudder, opened his eyes for the last time, and died, with Father cradling his head. An agonising, awful cry escaped from Father's lips, 'No! Nikki! No!' And he started to weep. We had never seen Father cry before, and we all cried with him.

We held a funeral for Nikki and Father buried him in the garden around the other side of the 'res'. We made a little head stone above the grave and said our goodbyes. Later on when we had come to terms with his death, Father said that he had probably caught a rat that had been poisoned. (Nikki had been wonderful at catching rats and throwing them up in the air and catching them in his jaws.)

On 28 November a particularly nasty air raid took place with thousands of incendiaries being dropped. A couple landed on the roof of my friend Peter Aze's house. His father, who was an ARP warden, climbed up a ladder to throw them down. But another warden saw the apparently unused ladder against a wall and took it to deal with other incendiaries. Charlie Aze shouted as loud as he could for help but, because of the din, no one heard him. He was up there until the raid was over and had a bird's eye view of the action. He saw the oil tanks ablaze at Mountbatten and a Sunderland Flying Boat that was burnt out to a skeleton in the Sound, which was terrible, yet spectacular.

Auntie Ivy was still very ill but hanging on, which surprised all the doctors and nurses at the City Hospital. Mother still saw her at least once a week.

In February 1944 I was taken ill again. Mother thought that I had a very bad cold, because of the time of the year. My throat was very sore and when she took a closer look and saw that it was a patchy grey colour, she became alarmed and immediately called for Dr Morris. My temperature had risen dangerously high and he diagnosed diphtheria, which was a killer disease.

Mother protested, 'But he's been immunised twice; the first one didn't take.'

'Well then, it won't be as bad as if he hadn't been immunised.'

I was sent by ambulance to the Scott Isolation Hospital. I remember being delirious and seeing a giant skeleton chasing me and then a cat swinging on a rope, as I sat in the gods at the Palace Theatre. I was put in an oxygen tent to help me breathe and then after three weeks was transferred to Lee Mill Cottage Hospital, which was eight or nine miles outside of Plymouth. This made it very difficult for Mother and Father to come and visit. Mother was also still visiting Auntie Ivy at least once a week, which took its toll on her with all the other things that she had to do.

However, they managed to come every Sunday by bus, which took a long time. When they did arrive they handed any presents for me to the nurses and then went along a veranda to see me through the window. We all had to lip-read. Rather disconcerting for them was that, as soon as I opened whatever they had brought, I would say, 'You can go home now.'

I was improving gradually and loved the view of the countryside around the hospital. I could see a farm not too far away and enjoyed watching the farmer plough his fields with two huge shire horses and seeing his sheepdogs running about. I wanted to stay in hospital forever.

After spending seventeen weeks in hospital I was told that I could go home in a week or two; the family was thrilled. Unfortunately I had pulled a piece of toenail off which had made it bleed. I had wrapped it in a dirty handkerchief and as a result developed impetigo. I came out in scabs which I then proceeded to scratch off until the nurses put my arms in splints. This made doing things very difficult especially if I wanted to eat a sweet Mother had brought me. (She made her own sweets and toffee.) I had to guide the sweet towards my mouth which usually missed and dropped down my neck. So I had to summon a nurse to place it in my mouth for me.

The final Sunday before I was to return to the cottage Mother brought Jean to see me. She was wearing her Sunday frock and some new patent-leather shoes. After looking through the window for a while she got bored and asked if she could play in the field that was just a short distance from the hospital and where Mother could see her. However, in no time at all she was back crying and, at once, Mother could see what the problem was, as well as smell it. She had slipped on the grass and landed in fresh cow dung. The hospital staff cleaned her up as best they could, but on the bus journey home, they received some hostile stares as the reek filled the bus.

The following week I went home, which was wonderful. Mother had put on a splendid tea and many of my friends came to see me. In August Father took Mother to hear Glenn Miller and his orchestra at the Odeon Picture House.

The winter of 1944 was cold and bleak and there was a heavy fall of snow. The fields were a good place to toboggan: we used pieces of corrugated metal. It was such good fun, except when we landed in the bog at the bottom of the slope. We also sat on a short stubby ladder, six of us at a time, and slid down the icy back lane. The 'res' was frozen over and one morning I saw a duck sliding around on it, unable to take off. I rushed in and got Father's air rifle and the first shot hit its wing, which made it flap around drunkenly. The second shot went right through its eye and killed it instantly. I felt very sorry for what I'd done. I managed to get the duck to the side and rushed to show Mother. She said, 'You cruel boy, what have you done?' I was sent to my room.

Father's attitude, however, was one of complete indifference, saying, 'Tomorrow take it to Hornes the butcher and see if they will buy it from you.'

The butcher gave me five shillings, after telling me off and saying that killing duck was against the law.

Father had no compunction about docking the tails of puppies for his friends, because they paid him to do it. I saw him tie a piece of string tightly around the puppy's tail and then cut it off with his sharp leather knife.

'Does it hurt them?' I enquired.

'Course it doesn't.'

'Why do they yelp then?'

'Go away and mind your own business.'

Father was not sympathetic at all when we children hurt ourselves. He used to say, 'Let me look at it.' When we showed him the cut or bruise he spat on it and said, 'There, that will make it better.' He usually laughed and we soon learned not to go to Father.

The children in the area used to come to see Father to have their baby teeth pulled out, with the consent of their parents. He had a good pair of pliers. He also used snail's blood to wash out eyes if anyone had got something in them. He pricked the shell with a pin and let the light blue blood run into the eye to flush out the foreign body.

The news on the wireless seemed to intimate that the war would be coming to a close in months rather than years. Mother was pleased as was Father, and they made plans to really enjoy this Christmas. Jean was now eleven and had joined the Girl Guides; I was nine and had joined the 11th Devonport Wolf Cubs; Pat was seven; and John Sylvanus was four and a half. With the exception of Jean, we all believed in Father Christmas. I had seen him at Stuart Herring's Christmas party and he had scared me stiff.

Father had been busy in the workshop making toys for the shop in Stoke village and had made quite a bit of money. He was unusually generous this year and gave Mother some extra for Christmas. She bought some real clotted cream from

Mallet's dairy in the ope, instead of skimming off the cream from the milk, as was her habit, and had been able to buy a few sweets from Spooner's sweet shop.

On Christmas Eve, Mother bathed us in front of the fire, using the hot water from the Ascot. She rubbed our chests with camphorated oil, then let us stay up a little later than usual to listen to the wireless. Then we went to our beds, excited as ever, with our pillowslips on our backs.

Father was propping up the bar of the Stoke Inn and had become rather drunk. He arrived home just before eleven o'clock in a foul mood and sat in front of the fire to have a smoke before retiring. Mother had been in bed for a good half-hour and heard him noisily climbing the stairs. 'Shush John, be quiet, you'll wake the children.'

Father retorted, 'Who's making a noise?'

She looked imploringly at him, 'Please, John.' She put her fingers to her pursed lips. Father grabbed her roughly and pushed her down on the bed. Jean heard the ruckus and came into their bedroom just as Father was shaking Mother by the shoulders. She picked up a wooden coat hanger from the dressing table and advanced towards Father. He looked round to see her and let go of Mother. He was very surprised and said, 'Go back to your bed immediately my girl.'

Mother took the coat hanger and brought it down across Father's shoulder with such a force that it broke in half. He let out a yell of pain and, before he could say anything, Mother said, 'Don't you ever push me again.'

Jean was crying and pushed herself between Mother and Father. He seemed to sober up and said, 'I didn't mean to push you, honest I didn't.'

Mother led Jean quietly back to bed and when she returned to her own bed Father was in a drunken stupor, snoring his head off. The rest of us were unaware of what had gone on and enjoyed our Christmas Day.

The day after New Years Day, about mid-afternoon when it was getting gloomy, there was a knock on the door of Auntie Ivy's flat in Park Street. The tenants in the other flat answered the door to see a telegram boy with a telegram in his hand, his bike propped up against the short wall outside. 'Telegram for Mrs Lambert.'

'I'm afraid that she's in the City Hospital, but her relatives live just around the corner at Reservoir Cottage.'

'I'll try there then.'

Mother saw the boy coming and wondered what it was all about. She rushed outside. 'I have a telegram for Mrs Lambert, but was told that she's in the hospital.'

'She is. I'm her sister. Could I take it to her?'

'I'm sorry, but I have to give it to the right person.'

'Do you know what it's about?'

'No, not really. Would you tell her that there is a telegram for her and that I will get it to the hospital as soon as possible.'

'Of course I will. I'll go this afternoon.'

'I'll take it back to the office then.'

The boy returned to the post office and was told to take it to the hospital. When he enquired at the porter's lodge where Mrs Lambert was he was directed to her ward. Mother and Father arrived at the hospital as the telegraph boy was leaving after handing the telegram to the matron. She was in a quandary about what to do. She didn't think that Ivy would be able to read it as she was so ill and some of her faculties were lacking. Mother and Father went to the matron's office and knocked on the door. They went in.

'Ah, Mr and Mrs Trevail,' she said, 'I have a telegram from the War Office for Ivy.'

'Yes we know, that's why we're here. We saw the boy earlier.'

The matron handed the telegram to Mother who took it with a slight tremble in her hands. Then she and Father went to Ivy's bedside. Ivy was sleeping peacefully so Mother decided not to wake her.

'Well open it then,' Father said.

'I don't really want to until she's awake.'

'I'll read it then.' Father took the telegram and ripped it open. Mother saw his jaw drop open and a look of disbelief came over his face. 'The ruddy blighter. I knew he'd come up smelling of roses.' Father had a grin like a Cheshire cat.

'What is it?' Mother asked. Father passed her the telegram.

MRS LAMBERT. STOP. THE WAR OFFICE IS PLEASED TO INFORM YOU THAT PRIVATE J.H.R. LAMBERT No 14645579 IS ALIVE. STOP. RETURNING HOME SOON. STOP.

There was a signature at the bottom, but Mother fell off the bed in a swoon, knocking a metal jug on the floor, which jolted Ivy awake. A nurse was soon on the scene and brought her round.

Mother said, 'Poor Ivy, after what you've been through.' She told Ivy the ecstatic news and saw that she understood.

'Why did they say he was killed?' Ivy rasped, her voice very weak and hard to hear.

Father said in an unusually compassionate voice, 'These things do happen from time to time.'

Mother and Auntie Ivy found the news very difficult to take in, because all of this time they had imagined him dead somewhere in Burma. Ivy was crying, so Mother and Father both put their arms around her to comfort her. Father seemed to have forgotten that he might catch something from Ivy.

'Tell him it wasn't my fault, Vi. I can't bear to see him.'

'Don't you worry, we'll see to it,' Father said.

Before they left the hospital they saw the matron and explained everything. 'Is there any way that he can be contacted to let him know that his wife is seriously ill and might die?' Mother begged.

'Leave it with me. This is an emergency and we can do something in these extreme cases, but we must act quickly, poor Ivy hasn't got much time left. I'll contact the War Office and tell them the situation.'

They thanked her and couldn't wait to get home to give us the news. We couldn't believe it and we all screamed and cried and jumped around hysterically.

'Uncle Jack's coming home!'

'When is he coming home?'

'Soon we think,' said Father.

None of us got any sleep that night thinking about seeing our dear Uncle Jack again.

Chapter 18

In April 1945 my friends decided that we would build a little fire near the place where Stuart had been impaled on the railings. We all had to ask our mothers for a potato so that we could have a bit of a picnic. Mother gave me one and said, 'Be careful of the fire.'

'Course I will,' I replied.

We managed to get a good blaze going and we pressed sticks through the potatoes to bake them in the embers. After about fifteen minutes a crowd of older boys from the area arrived on the scene to ask us what we were doing.

'I bet you don't know what we've got.' They were grinning at each other. 'You'd run a mile if we showed you.'

We all shouted, 'Please show us.'

None of us had a clue, so they showed us. The boys opened their hands and revealed some real live bullets. 'Wow! Where did you get those?'

'You all must promise not to say anything to anybody.'

We all shouted, 'Yes. We promise.'

They told us that they had found them in Central Park on the sight where some Americans had been billeted. The oldest boy said, 'If we throw them on the fire they'll go off. I saw it in a cowboy film.'

Someone else said, 'Better put some protection around the fire; we don't want anyone to get shot.'

We found some old rusty galvanised metal sheets and placed them around the fire. 'That ought to do it,' one of the older boys said.

By this time the fire had died down a little. They threw some of the bullets in the embers and we all waited expectantly. After what seemed a long time, there was a loud explosion and some of the embers flew up in the air. Then another went off. We all cheered. 'Everybody: get more wood for the fire,' someone shouted.

We all went searching for twigs and I saw just the right one, so I bent down to pick it up. A few more bullets exploded to another great cheer. But instantly I felt an excruciating pain in my right wrist and immediately a jet of dark red blood shot two feet up into the air. I let out a piercing scream, which got the attention of everybody. One of my friends grabbed me and rushed me up the lane to the cottage and pushed my wrist under the outside tap and turned it on full. This made it hurt even more and by this time I was howling in pain and agony. The water mixed with the blood poured down the drain.

Mother heard the commotion and came out. 'He's been shot Mrs Trevail; a bullet came out of the fire.' Mother tried to take in what was being said as she dragged me inside and wrapped a white tea towel around my arm and held it up as high as it would go. I had lost a lot of blood and was feeling cold and clammy. The blood began to seep through the towel and I was starting to feel faint. 'I've got to get him to the doctor right away,' said Mother.

The nearest doctor was a foreign one by the name of Colombo, who had a surgery in Molesworth Road. No one seemed to know where he had come from except that he was foreigner. Mother took me into his surgery. 'Vot haf ve got ere then?' Mother explained what had happened. 'Vy don you bois play in de parks and then you voud be all right?'

He looked at my wound, which had now stopped bleeding, and after washing it he placed some powder on the wound and stuck a plaster over it. I was relieved that I wasn't going to die but disappointed that I only had a small plaster to show for being shot. The doctor then shouted at me, 'Now I don vant to see you again.'

I was glad to leave the surgery. I went to bed when I got home, because I felt sick. The older boys with the remaining bullets threw them down a storm drain when they realised that they could be in trouble with the police. The doctor informed the local bobby, Mr Steer, Graham Steer's father, and he made some enquiries, but never quite got to the bottom of it. I recovered in a day or so.

Meanwhile Mother and Father had had to take John Sylvanus, who was now five years old, to see Dr Morris, as his limp had got progressively worse, He was also feeling listless and his knee was swollen. After a thorough examination the doctor said, 'I'm sure that John has tuberculosis in his right knee, but you must see a consultant to make sure. I'll refer you to one at Mount Gould Hospital. It is curable but it could take many years to heal.'

Mother and Father received an appointment letter from Mount Gould Hospital, explaining when they were to take him. It also said that they should bring a small case with pyjamas and toiletries. The boy didn't understand what was happening, but Mother and Father were extremely anxious.

They made their way to the hospital by bus and, when they arrived, entered the imposing gates. After reporting to reception they were shown to the consultant's room. A very nice looking man introduced himself. 'I'm Mr Robins and am a consultant specialising in TB. Please take a seat, do. And you must be Master John?' he said, smiling at John Sylvanus, who snuggled closer to Mother. 'We'd like to keep the boy in for a few days to conduct some tests, just to determine what the problem is.'

'What sort of tests?' Mother enquired.

'A tuberculin skin test. We inject the tuberculin into the body, just under the skin, and then wait for seventy-two hours to see what effect it has. If there is a swelling we measure it. Also we can take a biopsy of his knee and an X-ray.'

'I thought TB was in the lungs, not in a person's knee,' said Father.

'That is the usual site, but it can be anywhere in the body,' replied Mr Robins.

'I'll get sister to admit him. So would you like to say your goodbyes?'

Mother turned to John Sylvanus and said, 'The nice lady is going to put you in bed in a minute, and Mother and Father are going home to look after your brother and sisters. Now I want you to be a brave boy. We'll come and see you tomorrow.'

The sister came into the consulting room and spoke quietly to John Sylvanus. 'You kiss your mummy and daddy and we'll find a nice bed for you.'

After the kisses, he went like a lamb with the sister. Mother wept and Father supported her as they made their way home. The next day Mother visited John Sylvanus. He was very cheerful and not a bit distressed.

A few days later both Mother and Father saw Mr Robins again.

'Hello again,' he said. 'I've got the results of the tests and I'm afraid that he has a tubercular knee. We've put his leg in plaster up to his tummy. We'll have to keep him in hospital for quite a while, I'm afraid.'

'Oh dear, poor John Sylvanus.'

'This is going to take a long time to heal, and we'll eventually have to fit him with a calliper, in order to keep his leg stiff.'

'Please can we see him now?'

'Of course you can. I'll get a nurse to take you to him.'

'Thank you so much for your care and help,' Mother said.

'Yes, we're very grateful,' added Father.

The nurse took them to a ward of men and boys. John Sylvanus was sitting up in bed, looking at the pictures in a story book. Mother and Father went up and kissed him.

'How are you feeling, John?' Mother asked.

'My leg in plaster, look.' He pulled back the bed covers and showed them his leg encased in plaster of Paris.

'Oh, you poor boy. Does it hurt?'

'Not hurting, Mother.'

The nurse told them that he had settled in very well and that all the nurses adored him. 'Don't fret, he'll be well looked after,' she said, smilingly.

This was the first of many visits the family would make before John Sylvanus was allowed home.

Brother John had his leg in plaster of Paris from his foot to his stomach for many years and finally in a leg iron with a special boot. It didn't stop him doing anything and we all laughed to see him playing football and also riding a bicycle with one leg, his stiff leg, hanging down. When Mother bathed him she obviously took off the leg iron. We were afraid that he might bend his leg and do himself some damage; it was also withered as it was not being used. It eventually took seven years before it was fully recovered, though it was only a little smaller than the other leg.

The war was coming to an end. On 2 May Hitler and his mistress Eva Braun married, and only a few days later committed suicide. On 3 May Admiral Von Friedeburg and General Kinzel surrendered the army in the northern parts of Germany to Field Marshall Montgomery in the caravan that had been the latter's travelling headquarters. On 7 May Colonel Gustaf Jodl signed an unconditional surrender of Germany in a Rheims classroom. Because Russia, America and Britain wanted to announce the news simultaneously, 8 May was to be Victory in Europe (VE) day.

Jean had been on a trip to Mevagissey in Cornwall on that day and, as their train drew into North Road Station, the public address system announced the news. There was pandemonium with all the passengers laughing and shouting and embracing each other. Mother and Father and we children hugged each other at the good news. Our neighbours came out into the streets ecstatic and full of cheer, hardly daring to believe the good news. They danced with each other and were singing. It was a sight to behold. Everyone was laughing their heads off. Old differences were forgotten. And we were all glued to the wireless waiting for Churchill's speech.

To say that the feelings of the people were at a euphoric level was an understatement. Everyone was to have two days holiday and street parties were being organised all across the country. Our neighbours in Park Street and at Ann's Place formed a committee to plan the celebrations for a party the next day. Rations that had been hoarded for a rainy day were being taken from their hiding places. We helped to collect flags and bunting to drape in the streets. Mr Tallack put a tall white flag pole in his front garden and flew a Union Jack on it.

* * *

Jack had received the news that Ivy was very ill in the city Hospital. He was flown home by special dispensation and landed at RAF St. Mawgan in Cornwall. He was now on the train to Plymouth.

He had somehow managed to get a message to Mother and Father saying that he would be at the hospital at about 3.30, and would they be able to meet him there. My parents quickly got ready and caught the bus to the hospital. They were there at three o'clock and went to Ivy to tell her the news. 'Jack will be here soon to see you Ivy.'

Ivy was weeping, which started Mother off. Father had a large lump in his throat too. Then the matron came to the bedside to tell them that Jack was in her office. 'You stay with Ivy and I'll bring Jack,' Father said.

Father saw a thin, very sunburnt man in uniform, next to a kitbag with a bush hat on the top. It was undeniably his brother-in-law Jack Lambert. Jack got up and gave Father a hug. 'Thank goodness you are here Jack. It's wonderful to see you.'

'And you too John, I'm so glad to be home. How is Ivy?'

'Be prepared for the worst. She's very ill and you'll find it hard to recognise her.' Father very quickly explained all that had happened to Ivy, and how she came to be so ill.

'I want to see her now,' he said urgently.

The matron rushed in and said, 'She's failing fast and hasn't got much time Mr Lambert. We're amazed that she's survived this long.'

Uncle Jack looked desolate as a nurse took him to her bed that had a coloured screen around it. Mother heard the voices and came out. 'Oh Jack. You're here at last.' She hugged and kissed him through her tears.

Jack opened the screen and went inside. His entire being was overwhelmed, and he was in a state of catatonic shock and utter despair when he saw his beloved Ivy looking skeletal and almost bald. Her wonderful looks had gone and she looked very old. He held her hand and kissed her forehead. She managed to open her eyes for a brief instant when he squeezed her hand and gently whispered her name. There was a brief look of recognition and she managed a raspy, 'Is it really you Jack?'

'It is Ivy. I'm alive, and I've come to take you back home.'

She smiled a wan smile and lay there struggling to breathe. 'Will you forgive me?'

With tears streaming down his cheeks, his strong voice breaking, he said, 'I forgive you and I love you.'

'I never stopped loving you Jack. Even when I got that telegram.' She squeezed his hand, opened her eyes wide, and with a final shudder of her emaciated body, she died.

He kissed her forehead again and held her wasted body. 'Ivy! My Ivy!' he wailed.

He stayed with her until the matron led him back to her office. 'She's gone,' he said to Mother and Father.

Mother and Father consoled Jack as they left the hospital to return to the 'res' to tell us the sad news. We were on the one hand over the moon to see dear Uncle Jack, and on the other hand broken hearted to hear that Auntie Ivy had passed away.

Later that evening after we had gone to bed, Jack revealed that the matron had been able to get special dispensation for him to fly home because his wife was at the point of death. He also told them that he knew that he had been reported killed in action. Some Burmese peasants who were pro-British had found him in the jungle, barely alive. They had looked after him until he was able to be moved. Eventually they were able to contact the allies and he was taken to a hospital in Poona, India, to recover fully from his injuries.

They had supper and Mother made them all a mug of cocoa. They talked well into the night and made up a bed so that Jack could stay.

* * *

The next day the two streets were hives of activity. Trestle tables were obtained and placed in the middle of the streets. Chairs of all shapes and sizes were placed at the tables. White sheets, freshly washed and ironed, were draped over the tables. It looked wonderful.

Mother baked cakes and buns, as did all the other mothers. The food was laid out on the tables and it was as much as we could do to stop ourselves eating it. We had never in our lives seen such a bounteous spread. The celebrations began.

We children had races and won prizes. Everyone was laughing and there was a carnival atmosphere about the place. Someone had brought out a gramophone and was playing a Glen Miller record, which the adults were dancing to. But we were getting very impatient to eat, and at last at three o'clock we had permission to sit at the table. We all cheered and scrambled for a seat. The food tasted scrumptious. We had never seen so much food. We children filled our bellies so much so that some children were sick afterwards. I wasn't.

Uncle Jack was with us and he seemed to enter into the spirit of the celebrations, although we were all sad in our hearts at losing Auntie Ivy. We had a wonderful feast and there were a few toasts given. Father got up and made a speech.

'We have all been through an awful trial over the last six years, but at last the war in Europe is over and it won't be long before Japan surrenders.' Everyone cheered and clapped. He continued, 'We have to thank all those who gave their lives in this struggle for victory to make this day possible for us. I would like you to raise your glasses for my brother-in-law Jack Lambert who is here with us today and has just returned from India.'

Someone shouted, 'Three cheers for Jack! Hip hip hooray! Hip hip hooray! Hip hip hooray!' Everyone clapped and cheered.

We all had such a wonderful time and, late in the evening, we made our way to the 'res', all our arms entwined, looking forward to the days of peace that lay ahead and the stories that Uncle Jack would tell us.

Lightning Source UK Ltd.
Milton Keynes UK
UKOW04f2256220215

246654UK00002B/33/P